CREATIVE THOUGHTS PUBLICATIONS

PRESENTS

WHEN A RICH THUG WANTS YOU

AN URBAN LOVE TALE BY

PEBBLES STARR

www.jadedpublications.com

ARE YOU ON OUR EMAIL LIST?

Text BOOKS to 44144 to

be the first to hear about new releases, contests,

and giveaways!

LOOSELY BASED ON TRUE EVENTS…

This novel is a work of fiction. Any reference to real people, events, establishments, or locales is intended only to give the fiction a sense of reality and authenticity. Other names, characters, and incidents occurring in the work are either the product of the author's imagination or are used fictitiously, as are those fictionalized events and events that involve real persons. Any character that happens to share the name of a person who is any acquaintance of the author, past or present, is purely coincidental and is in no way intended to be an actual account involving that person.

ONE

Loud rap music thumped through the speakers of Club Indigo on a Friday evening, and the place was jam packed. Raelyn and her girls, Blue and Symba were among the crowd of club-goers as they shuffled to get to the empty seats at the bar. Though the place was filled to capacity, the three women still managed to stand out. Dressed in designer wear from their head to their thousand dollar shoes, you would've thought they were celebrities—or at least the wives of male celebrities.

Twice, Raelyn had been stopped and asked if she was a reality star from one of Atlanta's many hit TV shows. With a curt smile, she shook her head no, loving every minute of the overwhelming attention.

Rarely did Raelyn go out. As a matter of fact, she barely left the three bedroom luxury condo she lived in—thanks to her overprotective fiancée, Marlon Jetson aka Jett. He could put a teenage daughter's father to shame with how controlling he was.

Truthfully, Jett wasn't feeling the idea of Raelyn stepping out for the night. He hated whenever she went out parlaying with her attention-seeking girlfriends whom he'd warned her about hanging with.

Jett despised the thought of another nigga pushing up on what he considered was rightfully his. He'd taken Raelyn's virginity five years ago on her 17th birthday, and he would be damned if he let another motherfucker even take a whiff of her goods. Raelyn was his. She knew it. He knew it. And every nigga in a 200 mile radius knew it…Well…everyone except for the tall, dark chocolate, hunk checking her out from across the club.

Nicki Minaj's "*No Flex Zone*" poured through the speakers as Caesar, his partner Canyon, and a few of their closest associates held shit down in the VIP section. Although, he wasn't really the party type, Caesar was a firm believer in keeping up appearances.

A colorful array of women from all different races surrounded them, each one looking for a nigga that would change their life. Even with the lovely selection of women in his face, Caesar only seemed to have eyes for one.

Damn, shawty bad.

In the midst of staring at Raelyn, Caesar noticed a trio of women gawking at their section from across the club.

Whenever he and Canyon stepped out on the scene, everyone ate and drank for free. Small time hoodlums turned big time entrepreneurs they had no problem feeding the fam and anyone wanting to be associated. Finances were the least of their concerns.

Spend that shit without a care in the world. Ain't like you can take it with you when you gone. That had been their motto for years.

Using his index finger, Caesar beckoned the three sexy women to join them in VIP. Smiling from ear to ear, they quickly made their way over to the already crowded section. Champagne bottles popped and marijuana clouds filled the air. As usual, their camp had the place on lock.

As Raelyn navigated through the thick crowd of people, her gaze briefly connected with the guy who'd been peeping her swag. A flock of chicks surrounded him, but yet and still he seemed fixated on her.

Raelyn noted his tall, muscular physique, designer wear, and glowing jewelry. He was fine as hell, and judging from the cocky poise he held she was sure he knew it as well. The way his Givenchy tee hugged his broad chest and made his biceps look almost Hulk-like was hypnotic.

Must be a ballplayer or one of these new rappers out here, she thought.

As soon as Raelyn noticed they'd been keeping eye contact for a bit too long, she quickly tore her gaze away. The last thing she wanted was to give a nigga the impression that she wasn't already taken.

“Damn, I can’t believe it’s this packed in here!” Raelyn shouted over the blaring bass. She looked stunning that evening in a fitted red Chanel dress and Giuseppe sandals. Jett spared no expense when it came to spoiling her. In his mind, luxuries were the invisible leash he kept tied around his girl so she wouldn’t roam.

Standing at an even 5”7, Raelyn’s smooth, blemish-free skin was the color of honey. Her long, auburn hair was flat-ironed bone straight, and pulled up into a sleek ponytail which showed off her delicate features. Raelyn’s high cheekbones, mint-colored eyes, and piercing dimples made her look almost exotic. Breathtaking would have been an understatement if used to describe her.

Anytime Raelyn stepped in a room she commanded attention. There wasn’t a nigga around who didn’t stop what they were doing to check her out. And every insecure female made sure to check to see if their man was watching.

“Girl, tell me about it. You’d think the owner was giving away free bottles or some shit,” Blue joked.

At only twenty-one, Blue Davenport was the youngest of the trio and the most rambunctious at a mere 4’11. Blue’s fair skin was the color of French vanilla, and she wore her long wavy hair aqua blue. Fifty percent of her body was covered in tattoos, and the septum piercing she sported made her look fierce.

Once the girls finally made it to the bar, Symba was the first to order. "Let me get a double shot of Hennessey," she said, placing her custom made clutch on the surface.

At twenty-three, Symba was the eldest, and the most calm of the three. However, Raelyn was sure that her unquenchable thirst for liquor contributed to her docile personality. She didn't talk much about her personal life, and her girls were the closest thing she had to family.

Although Symba fronted like she didn't have a care in the world, she drank herself to sleep every night. And when she wasn't tossing back a shot, she was fucking promiscuously as if it were a hobby. Symba was to sex what an addict was to crack; but luckily her girls never judged her though and that's why she loved them.

Symba was a beautiful brown-skinned woman with plump lips and a fat ass that she always used to her advantage. Although, her many prospects kept her satisfied there wasn't a single man out there who possessed her heart.

Just seconds before Raelyn ordered her usual—Sex on the Beach—her secret admirer and his patnah approached her and her girls. "Hey, Jessica. Do me a favor and start a tab," Tall, Dark, and Handsome said to the bartender. "Anything they order's on me."

Symba and Blue smiled giddily at one another. There was nothing better to them than having complimentary drinks all night.

Raelyn, on the other hand, looked up and met the penetrating gaze of her admirer. He was even sexier up close in person. In fact, she was surprised he was able to break away from his herd of groupies for two minutes.

Damn, he smells so good too, Raelyn thought to herself.

"How you doin'? I'm Caesar," he said, extending his large hand. The diamond Rolex watch on his wrist sparkled beautifully. His attire was so flashy that Raelyn barely even recognized the foreign designer wear. She would be lying to herself if she said his swag wasn't on point.

"And I'm engaged," Raelyn smiled, holding up her ring finger. The $8000 round-cut ring sparkled beautifully. She was always ready to show it off at the drop of a dime, but never quick to admit that the piece of jewelry was in fact stolen.

Grinning slightly, Caesar held his hands up in mock surrender. "Aight then, Miss Lady. My aim isn't to step on anyone's toes. Just wanted to be the fiftieth dude tonight to tell you how beautiful you are."

Raelyn smirked, but held her composure. Compliments came to her naturally. However, something about hearing it from a well-dressed stranger made her blush just a little. “Thank you.”

Caesar smiled, revealing a perfect set of pearl white teeth. “Look, if you and ya girls—or you and ya man come through again, drinks on me. I’m the owner,” he told her. “It was nice meetin’ you, aight. You enjoy yaself.”

Raelyn smiled, clearly impressed by chivalry. “You too. And thank you again,” she replied sweetly.

“Always,” Caesar said before walking off.

On cue, his fine ass brown-skinned friend followed suit—but not before winking at Symba.

With how drop dead gorgeous Caesar was, Raelyn knew he wouldn’t have a problem finding the next chick. *Bitches nowadays are like vultures for a nigga with a little paper in his pockets.*

Caesar kept his cool as he swaggered off. He could still feel Raelyn’s eyes watching him even though she told him she wasn’t interested. Although he didn’t get any play, he refused to be a dick just because she had a nigga.

Money wasn’t shit to him; neither was getting pussy, and he was far from being careless with either. At twenty-six, Caesar was far more mature than niggas twice his age. A young boss, he looked and conducted himself as such. And one thing was for certain; leaders didn't sweat the small shit—especially women.

Maybe I'll run into her again under different circumstances, Caesar thought.

He'd put a seed in Raelyn's ear, and that was all that mattered at the end of the day. All he had to do was play his hand right the first time.

"Damn, Ray. You cold, bitch," Blue cackled. "That nigga was fine as fuck! And fresher than a new pair of kicks."

"*And* selfless!" Symba added, holding up her complimentary beverage. She loved a nigga that wasn't scared to break bread.

"Duly noted," Raelyn smiled. "But ya'll hoes must've forgotten that I gotta man at home—"

"Bitch, you've been wearing that rock for the past two years," Blue reminded Raelyn.

"Right! My damn bridesmaid's dress is collecting dust in the fucking closet," Symba teased. "You stay squawking about that wedding that ain't even happened yet—"

"It's *gonna* happen," Raelyn stressed.

"When?" Blue hounded. "'Cuz from the looks of shit, it seems like Jett put that rock on you just to prove a point."

Raelyn was now becoming annoyed. "And what point is that? Please enlighten me."

"That you're *his,*" Symba chimed in. "So niggas like the nice one you just passed up on don't stand a chance! I'm telling you, Raelyn, that motherfucker just wants to make a statement. I mean, think about it—"

"Look, I'm not trying to *think about it.* And I'm definitely not 'bout to do this with ya'll here," Raelyn waved them off. "I just wanna enjoy myself, okay. Can we do that?" She then lifted her glass, motioning for a toast.

"Hell yeah," Symba smiled. Beef between them never lasted long, and most times it was completely nonexistent. The three friends were tighter than a virgin female.

"Shit, I'll drink to that," Blue sang, clinking her shot glass against theirs.

TWO

It was nearing 2 a.m. when Raelyn finally returned home. As usual, she found Jett in the living room chilling with his boys, Roman and Ace. They were holding the sectional down while watching first quarter of the game. Jett was so glued to the massive television screen that Rae doubted he even heard her enter.

She and Jett rented a beautiful high rise condo in the prestigious Buckhead. It was a total step up from the roach infested apartment they used to rent a few years ago in Jonesboro. Back then Jett's money was nowhere near as long as it was now, but Rae loved him and she was willing to go through hell and high water if that meant being together.

After tossing her clutch on the granite countertop, Raelyn walked over to Jett and placed a kiss on his temple from behind. She had long accepted his less than reputable career as a jack boy.

For over ten years, Jett had been making a living off running up in stash houses and taking everything from guns, cash, jewelry, and dope. Hell, even Raelyn's engagement ring was the property of an unsuspecting victim.

As Jett grew older, his love and greed for making cash increased. Because of his extensive list of enemies, he and Rae moved a lot around the city to keep a low profile.

Truthfully, Raelyn never agreed with how Jett earned his money. It was risky and flat out dangerous, but she couldn't argue with the fact that he provided for them. The illegitimate son of a pimp, Jett had an insatiable thirst for making cold hard cash at any and all costs.

Raelyn frowned at the beer cans and cocaine lines on the glass coffee table. She'd vowed to herself that she would never ever touch a single drug—and Jett wouldn't dare let her even if she tried. Much like any couple, they had their own set of morals and values. And it wasn't like Jett planned on changing his anytime soon.

"Hey, babe," Raelyn greeted. "Who's playin'?" she asked, although she could care less about football.

Jett was the typical pretty boy with caramel skin, light brown eyes, and thick lips. At 6'2, he was ripped like a NBA basketball player. Tattoos covered every inch of Jett's torso with Raelyn's name written in bold cursive lettering across his collarbone.

In high school, every chick wanted Jett and every dude wanted to be cool with him. He was known to everyone as the charming bad boy, and Rae was the good girl who fell right into his clutches. Back then, she was a freshman cheerleader and Jett was a senior on the football team with a rap sheet longer than the Bill of Rights.

Raelyn—like every other girl in high school—had a crush on Jett but figured he was out of her league. Besides, he'd never paid her any real attention. At least not until the morning he accidentally bumped into her in the hallway. The impact was hard enough to make her textbooks drop to the floor. Simultaneously, they knelt down to collect the books while Jett apologized profusely.

When their hands brushed against each other's, an electric shock jolted through their bodies. Jett wasted no time staking his claim before one of the other horny ass school boys got to her first. The rest was history after that.

Suddenly, Jett latched onto Raelyn's wrist quickly snapping her back to her horrific reality.

"Bitch, don't hey babe me? Fuck was you at? I done called you 'bout four gat damn times. You know how I feel about you stayin' out past midnight," he said, his eyes bloodshot and red rimmed. A tightly rolled joint hung from the corner of his dark lips as he spoke. Jett was high and tripping as usual. His paranoia always made him believe his girl was up to something.

Just six months shy of graduating and going on to play college ball, Jett lost his scholarship after testing positive for drugs. Dropping out of school altogether, he'd traded in his dreams for a life of crime. Over the years his drug usage increased, slowly diminishing his once tolerable personality.

Every day Raelyn asked herself why she put up with him, but the fact of the matter was she loved him. Not only that, but her upper-middle class parents had turned their backs on her after she dropped out of high school to play full-time wifey to Jett.

Upon being accepted into the prestigious Howard University, Rae unexpectedly got knocked up. What she didn't know was that Jett had been poking holes in the condom in an attempt to keep her from leaving. After choosing a life with Jett instead of an education, Raelyn's parents dismissed her, allowing her to learn from life on her own. After all, what was a better teacher than mistakes?

Two months pregnant, a young and naïve Raelyn moved in with Jett, completely unaware of her fate. Over time, she quickly discovered how controlling he was. Raelyn barely made it to her second trimester when she suffered a miscarriage. By then her once in a lifetime opportunity was gone and she was stuck with Jett.

Raelyn quickly snatched her arm away in irritation. Some things never changed. "Let go of me, Jett. The last time I checked I was grown. I shouldn't have to check in with you for every little thing I do—"

WHAP!

Raelyn's sentence was cut short after a brutal slap to the face. The blow was so sudden that it sent her stumbling backwards, causing her to nearly twist her ankle in her heels.

"Aye, man, chill," Ace said, rushing to Raelyn's defense. "That shit's uncalled for, blood. Fuck's wrong wit'chu? " This wasn't his first time seeing Jett strike Rae, and he doubted it would be his last. Still, Ace couldn't stand idly by and watch his boy manhandle his woman—especially when he was secretly feeling her.

Jett ignored Ace as he continued to stare daggers at Raelyn. "You know why that shit happened, right?" he asked casually.

"Fuck you, Jett," Raelyn muttered, clutching her stinging cheek. She didn't have the energy to fight back; especially when last month's bruises had just healed.

Rae never felt more humiliated than being hit on in front of Jett's friends. Completely embarrassed, she rushed to their master suite in tears.

"I done told ya ass about talkin' to me like I'm one of ya bitches," Jett yelled after her. He then turned towards Ace. "And nigga, I done told you about intervenin' in my shit, bruh. My house, my lady. You just a guest in this mufucka. Remember dat shit—"

"Yeah, whatever my nigga. Fuck you," Ace waved him off. Jett was the most arrogant shit talker he knew, but after years of friendship he was used to it.

Raelyn closed the bedroom door behind herself in order to have some privacy. She was the only woman she knew whose man treated her like she was his underage daughter—or better yet his property. Although she wasn't cool with Jett putting his hands on her, Rae was used to him flipping.

After stepping inside the adjoined bathroom, Raelyn headed to the vanity to survey the damage. Her skin was so light that she bruised incredibly easy. *The things I endure in the name of love*, Rae thought to herself.

"I don't even know why I put up with this shit," she muttered, wiping off her MAC foundation.

"You know why…," Jett suddenly said, walking up behind her. He'd entered the room so quietly she barely heard him come in. When Jett reached Raelyn, he wrapped his toned arms around her slim waist.

"Move, Jett. I'm not in the mood," Rae said, continuing with the task of cleaning of her face. Just the sight of him at the moment made her sick.

Jett slowly took the wet cloth from her and turned Raelyn around to face him. Any traces of anger quickly vanished, and his eyes were now filled with lust. “You so damn sexy when you mad,” he said.

“What do you want?” Rae asked, a smile forming in the corner of her lips. Tender moments like those came after every argument.

“To remind you why you put up wit’ a nigga…”

Suddenly, Jett lifted Raelyn up and placed her on the sink’s marble countertop. Strategically sliding between her legs, he moved her silk purple panties to the side. She was drenched well before his fingers even touched her moist clit.

“Pussy stay wet even when you mad at a nigga,” Jett noted before tasting her juices. After sucking the nectar clean off his index finger, he slid it back inside her soaking wet slot. No matter how bad, or how often they fought, Rae always succumbed to Jett sexually. Since a teen, he’d had that effect on her. Dick dizzy and in love, he had the twenty-two year old wrapped right around his finger.

Raelyn shivered as Jett softly pinched and rubbed her pearl. He knew just how to touch her and how much pressure to apply. After five years, he’d learned every special place and every way to turn Rae on.

Curving his finger upward, Jett tickled her spot until he finally felt her pussy muscles contract.

"You like that?" he whispered, placing fervent kisses along her jawline.

"*Oh, shit,*" Rae moaned after he slipped a second in. "Yes!"

Gently grabbing a hold of her throat, Jett kissed Raelyn passionately. His fingers continued to work magic inside her walls, making her kitty wetter with each small stroke.

Raelyn's cheeks turned bright red as her toes curled in ecstasy. "*Oooh*, shit, Jett!" she whimpered. "I'm about to…"

Before Raelyn could even finish, she squirted her juices all over Jett's hand and the lower half of his tee.

Jett chuckled softly—proud of his work—before removing his wet shirt. Raelyn's legs were still quivering when he slid back in between them. She hadn't moved from the spot she was in and her mouth was still slightly agape. Jett hadn't even piped Raelyn, and yet he'd left her speechless.

There ain't another nigga alive that's gon' do her better than I can, he thought arrogantly. Rae was his prized possession, and as long as he kept her in line he figured he didn't have shit to worry about.

With nothing left to say, Jett left the room as quietly as he had come. Raelyn was then left alone to her own troublesome thoughts.

You know why you put up with it, the tiny voice in the back of her mind whispered. *He's the love of your life…*

THREE

"Are you following me?" Symba asked, a slight smile tugging on her lips. She thought about hiding the bottle of Absolut but decided against it. Hell, everyone in the package store was there for the same reason.

"And if I am?" a smooth, deep voice replied.

A wide smile spread across Symba's face after noticing Canyon's fine ass from the club. His boy, Caesar was nowhere to be found, so Symba figured her assumption was correct.

"Well, I would hope you have a lot more courtesy to speak rather than to just tail me where ever I go—"

"Whoa. Whoa. Whoa," the dimpled, brown-skinned cutie replied. "Who said anything about tailin' you, Miss Lady?" He raised a thick, sleek eyebrow and Symba's pussy immediately jumped behind the thin fabric of her dress. As usual, she was pantiless, and ready for the first big dick that came her way.

Symba was so turned on by his sexiness that she was tempted to take him down an empty aisle and fuck him on site. Most of her sex rendezvouses were usually like that. Truth be told, they could get even wilder and ratchet depending upon her mood.

"I mean, don't get me wrong. You bad and all…but it's mere coincidence. Hell, I ain't ever been no hound, ma."

Symba fake-yawned a sigh of boredom. "Yeah, yeah. Whatever you say."

"You talk a lot of shit, I see," Canyon smirked. "What's yo' name anyway?"

"Symba," she smiled.

Canyon's heart instantly skipped a beat. He had a weakness for chocolate girls—especially feisty ones. "Symba," he repeated, admiring the way it rolled off his tongue. Eyeing the length of her curvy body, he also couldn't help but wonder how she felt rolling off his tongue. "I like that," he told her. "My name's Canyon."

"Pleased to meet you," Symba said.

"Likewise. So what'chu gettin' into now? I see you rollin' solo and shit."

"Actually, I'm 'bout to call it a night," Symba told him, holding up the bottle of Absolut.

"Aww, come on now. It ain't never no fun drinkin' alone," Canyon said. "You need to let ya boy slide through. I could bring us somethin' to twist up and we could just chill and get to know each other," he told her.

Symba seductively bit down on her bottom lip. Canyon was just what the doctor had ordered. "I like the sound of that," she said.

"Cool. Slide me ya number right quick."

***

Blue quietly entered her two bedroom apartment in Atlantic Station. She was slightly tipsy, but held her composure well. To her dismay, damn near every single light was on inside so she knew Deon was awake.

I swear this nigga stay running up the electricity bill like he pays for shit, Blue complained to herself.

After kicking off her platform red bottom heels, Blue padded barefoot to the master bedroom.

Sprawled out across the king size bed was Deon Atkinson, flipping through cable channels without a financial care in the world.

Broke motherfucker, Blue seethed.

She and Deon had been dating for the past three years. Back when they'd first met, he was on his shit; working a good paying corporate job and pushing a 2012 Maserati Gran Turismo. Every other month he took Blue on exotic vacations and spoiled her to no avail.

Life was great all up until Deon was unexpectedly laid off without so much as a notice. Apparently, the company he was employed with was hemorrhaging money, and forced to let a few of their best workers go.

Instead of getting out and finding the next best thing, Deon fell into a depressing slump. And to make matters worse, he picked up a nasty gambling habit. Everyone—including Blue's no-nonsense mother—lectured her about getting rid of his no good ass. But Blue loved him unconditionally, broke or not.

What type of bitch would I be if I left my man hanging high and dry just because he's down on his luck, Blue would often argue. Back then it made sense, but now she wasn't so sure. Deon lacked both drive and ambition, and Blue didn't know how much longer she could take care of both of them.

"Um, *hello*?" Blue asked, standing in the doorway of her bedroom. She'd been posted there for several seconds while Deon acted like he didn't see her.

"Oh, what's up?" he greeted nonchalantly. His bare feet were propped up on Blue's favorite $3,500 Adrienne Landau Chinchilla throw. It was a decorative gift from a friend that was meant for display only. But now Deon was using the expensive pillow as a foot stool. "Aye, did you get that for me?" he asked, not once looking in her direction.

"Did I get what?" Blue asked, now in a sour mood.

"What'chu mean 'what'? I asked you to cop me a $20 scratch off from the gas station—"

"Deon, I barely got money for all the bills. Let alone your stupid lottery tickets," Blue snapped. "If you wanna waste your money on that bullshit, don't do it on my expense. I've told you that already. Besides, there's never any fucking money in those things—"

"Bullshit. I won $500 once," Deon argued.

"That was *once*— a year ago—after you brought $260 worth with your unemployment check. Remember that? You do the math."

"Man, whatever. Miss me with that attitude shit," Deon said. "Besides, you got money to fuck off on clubs with ya girls."

"Correction," Blue said, holding up a pink stiletto nail. "I have money for *me*. Money *I* work hard for. How *I* choose to spend it is no concern to you since you *aren't* the one earning it, Deon."

"So that's what all this shit boils down to, huh? Money?"

Blue snatched the expensive throw from underneath Deon's feet and placed it back on the top shelf in her closet. "You tell me," she retorted.

"Man, act like you know a nigga," Deon said. "I'm da same mufucka that was takin' you to Turks and Caicos for ya birthday and shit. I had money."

"Exactly," Blue agreed. "*Had*."

Deon made a face in disgust after her comment. "And you *had* a lil' respect for yaself once upon a time," he retaliated. "Why the fuck you dressed like you tryin' to get in da club for free."

Blue looked down at her own attire then back at Deon. His Gemini ass was something else. "Quit playin', nigga. You know I'm untouchable. Anyway, you the one who brought me this fit," she reminded him.

Deon tried his best to front. Deep down, he knew Blue looked sexy as hell in a black tight-fitting leather two-piece…but he wouldn't dare give her the benefit of the doubt. His pride wouldn't allow him to. He simply couldn't fathom the thought of a whole bunch of slime ball ass niggas pushing up on his precious Blue. After all, it wasn't like she couldn't up and leave him for the next nigga, and that's exactly what his insecurities stemmed from.

Blue didn't understand Deon at all. He was cute as hell with mocha skin, chestnut eyes, and a toned physique. But ever since he'd been down on his luck, Deon was ugly as hell on the inside. Blue quickly learned that good looks—and love—could only go but so far.

"Why the hell you starting with me this late, D?" Blue asked, taking a seat on the edge of the bed. She had just gotten home, and already her man was antagonizing her. Sometimes she regretted the decision of moving in together. Maybe then, she wouldn't be taking care of a grown ass man.

Deon opened his mouth to respond, but was suddenly cut off by loud knocking on the front door. "Who dat?" he asked curiously.

Blue sucked her teeth and stood to her feet. She wasn't expecting any company, so she had no idea. "I don't know. Lemme see. Maybe it's one of the girls," she told him on her way out the room. Occasionally, Symba would accidentally leave her purse in Blue's car after a night of drinking.

I know this careless ass bitch ain't trippin' again, Blue said, smiling to herself.

Sashaying across the living room, she headed towards the large wooden front door. As soon as Blue opened it, her mouth automatically fell open.

FOUR

Blue wasn't expecting to see the tall, attractive cinnamon colored brother standing in front of her. As a matter of fact, it was the same person who'd brought her the Chinchilla fur Deon had been using as a foot rest.

"Zachariah, what are you doing here?" Blue hissed in a tone low enough for only the two of them to hear. She and Zac had started messing around last summer, and even though he knew she had a man, he still caught feelings.

When they first met he'd splurged on her and her girls back when she met him in Miami during Symba's birthday trip. The rendezvous was supposed to be a one-time thing, but Blue found herself fucking with him whenever he came in to town for business.

Although Blue loved Deon, sometimes she got tired of remaining faithful to a broke ass, bitter nigga. Once in a while, she craved a little pipe from someone who'd appreciate her twice as much—and who better to deliver than a nigga with ten inches of curved, thick dick and a legitimate job?

Shit. Why is he here, Blue asked herself. Now wasn't the time or place to be thinking about sex.

"Ignoring my calls and texts won't make me disappear, Blue," Zac said, apparently reading her mind. The look of desperation on his face made him almost look vulnerable. Zac was drop dead gorgeous with cinnamon skin, square jaw, and bedroom eyes. However, it was those thick lips that made Blue weak in the knees at first glance.

"Blue, who the fuck is that?!" Deon hollered from inside.

Zac's eyes wandered over Blue's shoulder into her apartment. When he didn't see anyone he looked back at Blue for answers.

"Blue?" Deon called out again.

Blue opened and closed her mouth several times. She was in complete shock at the sight of Zac standing on her doorstep.

Damn! Blue's conscience screamed. *If only the circumstances were different.*

All of a sudden, she heard Deon's footsteps approach her from behind…

FIVE

"Aye, bruh, what took you so damn long?" Caesar hollered out the window of his silver fully loaded 2014 Audi Spyder. He started to hound his nigga until he noticed the fine ass chocolate sister behind him.

This nigga, Caesar thought to himself shaking his head.

He and Canyon had been boys since the sand box, and now 20 years later, they were causing twice as much hell. At only twenty-five and twenty-six, the young pair were making moves and breaking bread with the international drug trade business they ran together.

Caesar and Canyon's come-up redefined the phrase "*Started from the Bottom Now We Here*". Back when most young niggas were picking their noses and playing Nintendo, Caesar and Canyon were out on the block putting in work with corner boys twice their ages. Both the children of drug addicted parents, the young friends had to get it how they lived if they wanted to survive—and hustling was what ultimately fed them.

Caesar, the brains of the operation, was the more levelheaded one. A year older than Canyon, he was a bit wiser and did most of the major decision-making in their organization. He also handled the money laundering, investing in small businesses around the city—one being the club he met Raelyn in.

Canyon, on the other hand, was a bite more reckless, but had settled down a lot over the years. He was the flamboyant one; the guy who always had to have the nicest car, fanciest crib, flashiest jewelry, and baddest bitch. He was an ole cocky, arrogant motherfucker who loved to brag, but he'd definitely earned his rights to the title.

Canyon was the talker and Caesar was the observer. For years, that was always how the duo had been.

"My fault, bruh," Canyon said. "I—uh—ran into a friend and we had to politic. Shit, you know." His tone was nonchalant, almost as if his lengthy absence wasn't a big deal. The woman behind him giggled and shook her head as she headed towards her Kia.

Seems like every thot I know owns a Kia, Caesar thought to himself in crude amusement.

The Game's "*Ali Bomaye*" bumped through his custom speakers and made the gravel vibrate. Ceasar fucked with Compton rapper heavy—personally and music wise.

Caesar watched as Canyon climbed inside his red and black Bugatti Veyron which was parked right next to his ride. He'd followed his homeboy to pick up some Garcia Vegas before they headed to the next spot.

Every other night they ran through the city, spending cash that came and went as frequently as the women.

Caesar couldn't even sweat his patna since he'd killed time by daydreaming about Raelyn. Too bad shit didn't go as planned.

Be like that sometimes, he thought. However, there was something about Raelyn that Caesar found irresistible.

Everything about her was bad; from her skin tone to the sexy ass Marilyn Monroe beauty mark on her cheek. Physically, "Ms. Engaged" was Caesar's type…but she was too stuck on buddy to give a real nigga the time of day.

Caesar took one last look at Symba before she climbed into her vehicle and started the ignition. For a split second he was tempted to pass his number on to her to give to her girl, but decided against it. The last thing Caesar wanted was to look like he was pressed or coming on too strong. Besides, thirstiness wasn't a good look. A nigga like him had a reputation to uphold to.

***

Raelyn was painting her toes and listening to Pandora when her cellphone vibrated on the nightstand.

"Hello?" Rae answered. She plugged one ear to block out Jett and his boys rooting for the Falcons. Knowing them, they had probably placed bets and the whole 9.

Raelyn was greeted with loud background noise before she even heard her friend's voice. "Rae, you there? Look, I need you to come right now!"

"Is everything okay?" Raelyn whispered into the receiver. The urgency in Blue's voice left her alarmed.

"I—Look, some shit just popped off and I need you here ASAP!" With that said Blue disconnected the call and tended to the matter at hand.

Closing her phone, Rae quietly stood to her feet and tiptoed towards the bedroom door. After cracking it open slightly, she listened in to see what Jett was up to. Second quarter obviously had him and his boys' attention. They even had a comment for every play.

This nigga will flip if he comes back and sees me gone, Rae thought. *I guess I'll just have to be back before the game is over*.

Grabbing up her clutch and heels, Rae silently tiptoed out the bedroom door and into the hallway. Suddenly, she hated the fact that they lived in a condo instead of a house. A back door would've been so convenient to slip through.

"Ha! Ha! Ha! Fuck I just tell you, nigga?!" Jett hollered, clapping his hands loudly after a touchdown. Football and strippers were the only things that could get him that amped.

As Rae crept towards her front door, she could hear her girls' voices in the back of her mind.

Leave that crazy, overprotective ass nigga alone.

Girl, when you gon' drop that dude? I'm telling you he's no good for you.

Blue and Symba never hid their obvious disdain for Jett. They didn't appreciate how he treated her, and his career choice offered the furthest thing from stability. Of course, the sentiment was mutual on Jett's end. Raelyn was torn.

Jett had her head gone. He was all she'd ever known.

Raelyn's bare feet glided across the dark hardwood floors as she continued to the front door. Suddenly, Ace looked over at her, and their eyes connected for several seconds. A strange feeling took over Raelyn, but she quickly brushed it away before sliding out the front door.

Talk about reliving your youth, she thought.

SIX

"Give me one mufuckin' reason why I shouldn't pop this fuck nigga?!" Deon screamed, waving his polished Glock in the air. "You really must've lost yo' fuckin' mind, Blue! I can't 'een believe you would step out on your boy!"

Zac didn't seem the least bit phased by threats. In fact, he looked amused. "That's the problem," he chuckled. "You a boy. Blue needs a man—"

"Zac! One thing I *don't* need is you instigating. Or telling me what I need," Blue snapped. Standing in between the tall men, she tried her best to keep the two from tearing each other apart.

Where the fuck are my girls, she asked herself. *I don't know how much longer I can keep these niggas from killing each other.*

"Well, maybe I should let *you* tell him what you need," Zac continued. "'Cuz if memory serves me right, you wasn't happy last I checked. As a matter of fact, you told me to wait until you were able to break things off smoothly. Well, Blue, I'm tired of fuckin' waitin'," Zac admitted. "I'm tired of goin' to sleep every damn night, knowin' you sharin' the same bed with this clown—"

"Zac, enough!" Blue yelled. Though his words touched her, now wasn't the time or the place.

Truthfully, Blue had no intentions of leaving Deon any time soon. She loved him, and she hated that her messiness was finally catching up with her. Zac was a good guy and all, but her heart already belonged to another.

"Aye, what da fuck this nigga talkin' 'bout, Blue?" Deon fired off on his girl. His pride was now wounded, and he was two seconds from putting a bullet in Zac's dome. He'd already shown the ultimate disrespect by popping up unannounced and airing out him and Blue's affair. Deon was liable to kill the motherfucker if he didn't shut his mouth soon. As a matter of fact, it was by the grace of God that he didn't pull the trigger already.

"Deon, I can explain," Blue pleaded. "But first I need you to put the gun down—"

"Nah, first I need you to look me in the eyes and tell me you ain't fuck this nigga," Deon said, voice laced with emotion. "Tell me this mufucka crazy, Blue. Tell me you don't know this nigga! Tell me this dude talkin' out da side of his neck and he don't mean shit to you."

"Then she'd be telling you a lie," Zac chimed in.

WHAM!

Deon punched the shit out of Zac, causing him to stumble backwards into the wall. "Nigga, you showed up at my crib claimin' you fucked my bitch?!" he screamed, spit flying from his mouth. "Fuck you thought?! Shit was finna be gravy?"

Blue quickly rushed in front of Deon to keep him from hurting Zac. He was a hood nigga with a mean streak, and had no problem putting a motherfucker in their place—especially over his girl.

Zac, on the other hand, had been raised with a silver spoon in his mouth. His parents came from wealth, and Blue doubted he'd ever been in one serious altercation. Honestly, his good guy demeanor was what attracted her to him. All of her life, she'd been into rough necks, so creeping with Zac was like a breath of fresh air.

He was kind, considerate, sweet, passionate, and selfless with his earnings. Had the circumstances been different, Blue would've gladly run off into the sunset with him. But sadly, they weren't. Blue was Deon's girl.

Had his ass waited for my got damn texts instead of showing up uninvited, none of this shit would be happening, Blue thought.

"Baby, you're right. He wasn't thinking at all," Blue said in Zac's defense. "You know that. And you don't have shit to prove to me, him, or yourself. So just stop…This is crazy. We can talk about it."

Zac wiped the blood off his bottom lip, and struggled to regain his balance. He couldn't believe she was actually taking Deon's side. The same nigga she'd bitched and complained about for nearly a year. The same one she said made her unhappy.

"You wrong, Blue. I'm thinking clearer than I've ever been...," he spoke up. "It was a mistake even coming here." Ego wounded, Zac headed towards the front door in disappointment.

I can't believe I actually thought she was ready for something real, he told himself.

Zac had made the mistake of falling for Blue and now it was too late to undo it. Good pussy had a way of making a nigga think recklessly.

"You damn right it was a mistake," Deon said after him.

Blue felt like shit as she watched Zachariah leave the apartment. Seconds later, her girls rushed inside—late as all hell.

"What the fuck is going on in here?" Symba asked with Rae hot on her heels.

It seemed like every other weekend the girls were bailing each other out of shit. The trio was condemned by drama.

"Yo' mufuckin' ass just disrespected me for the last time. That's what's going on," Deon said, his dark eyes focused on Blue. "Matter fact, I'm out this bitch. You want these niggas in the street? Have at it, hoe."

"Deon, no," Blue reached out for him, but he quickly moved past her. "Deon, wait! Don't go!"

After sliding on his Retro Jordans, Deon stormed out, slamming the front door behind him. The impact was so strong that a frame on the wall dropped and shattered.

"Fuck you then!" Blue yelled after him. Truth be told, if her girls weren't there, she would've broken down in tears.

"Well, damn," Symba said, slipping a small bottle of Absolut from her purse. After unscrewing the cap, she took a huge swig and then passed it to Blue.

"I'm sorry we're tardy to the party," Rae said, looking around at the small mess.

"Yeah, me too," Symba agreed. "I hate missing out on good drama."

Raelyn cut her eyes at Symba and frowned. "You can be so unsympathetic. It sickens me."

Symba playfully flipped Rae off.

"I need to get the fuck outta here and get some fresh air," Blue said in between whizzes. "Who's down for a nightcap?"

Rae opened and closed her mouth several times as she tried to think of an excuse without being honest. "I—Jett—"

"Bitch, fuck that nigga," Blue waved her off. "That motherfucker ain't got you on house arrest. I'm going through some shit right now and I need you by my side tonight. Shit, Rae, I just broke up with my dude for goodness sake!"

"Girl, bye! You break up with Deon every other week."

It was true. Whenever Blue and D fell out, he ran back to his mama—who filled his head with blasphemy—only to run back home after several days. Regardless of the way Mrs. Atkinson felt about Blue, her dear son just couldn't stay away.

His ass will be back, she thought to herself. *He always comes back.*

***

Compound was more packed than a Weezy concert that night. Apparently, a few celebs were in town and everyone wanted a small piece of the fame. It was nearing 1 a.m. when Rae, Symba, and Blue traipsed through the busy club as rap music blared loudly through the speakers.

On the drive over, Symba had reluctantly sent Canyon a text letting him know they needed to put a rain check on their evening. She wasn't all too thrilled about passing up on an opportunity to get some new dick, but she knew her girl Blue needed her. Whenever one of them had issues in the relationship department, they all went out and sought entertainment to take their mind off the B.S. at home.

"I wonder what's up with that VIP," Blue said, eyeing the space right next to the celebs. She and Symba looked over at each other in silent understanding. They had no issues with flirting their way into VIP, and were willing to do whatever it took. Raelyn, on the other hand, was a bit more modest.

Instead of following behind her girls, Raelyn hesitated. "I'm gonna run to the bathroom ya'll," she said over the loud music.

"Girl, please. You ain't 'bout to do shit but check in with your probation officer," Symba teased. "Gone head. You know where to find us."

Fucking thots, Raelyn jokingly said to herself. After they disappeared into the thick of the crowd, Rae headed towards the bar. First she needed a drink to take her mind off the stress they didn't know existed in her life.

I don't even feel like going back home and dealing with this nigga, Rae said to herself. She was still somewhat upset with Jett for putting his hands on her. At some point the shit had to stop…for the sake of their happiness and well-being.

Raelyn didn't know how much longer she could take the mental and physical abuse. Although she loved Jett, she wanted him to change. But like her mother used to tell her as a child, 'some people were stuck in their ways.'

As soon as Raelyn reached the bar, she plopped down in an empty stool, and started fishing in her clutch for her cell. *Let me at least see if he texted me.*

"Well, well, well," a familiarly deep voice spoke up. "What are the odds of running into each other twice in the same day?"

SEVEN

Raelyn immediately looked up and saw the same pair of piercing brown eyes from earlier. She recognized Caesar's expensive cologne before she did anything else.

"Not really…Atlanta's a small city..."

Damn, this chick is playing hard to get, Caesar thought. However, he didn't mind. He loved a challenge—especially a good one.

"Then that means the chances are even smaller. As a matter of fact, it might even be fate," he smiled.

"Or pure coincidence," Rae said matter-of-factly. Though on the outside she was giving him the runaround, Rae was screaming on the inside. *Damn, why does he have to be so fine*? Raelyn even found herself battling with keeping her composure.

Caesar chuckled and shook his head, revealing the sexiest set of dimples. His deep chocolate skin was so smooth and perfect that it almost looked Photoshopped. His teeth were just as immaculately white as she remembered.

"Some coincidences can be favorable," Caesar told her.

Damn, he has the type of face you wanna go to sleep and wake up next to every morning, Rae's conscious blurted out.

Raelyn shook the dangerous thoughts from her mind. “Maybe…”

Caesar sloshed around his beverage and smiled. “Yo’, no offense but you the most uptight bride-to-be I’ve ever met. You don’t even shoot a nigga down the nice way,” he laughed.

Raelyn couldn’t stop the giggle from escaping. “Whose fault is it that you keep trying?” she laughed.

“Can’t blame a nigga for bein’ persistent,” Caesar said. “You give that effect.”

“Look, it’s nothing personal...really. I’m usually not so pointed.” Rae then turned to face her charming admirer. *I bet he never has to deal with relationship problems. Not when he probably could have any chick he wanted.* “To keep it real, I haven’t had the best night,” she admitted in a low tone. “I hardly feel like being here.”

“Well damn. I’m sorry to hear that, ma,” Caesar apologized. “I really wish I could do somethin’ to change that. I never got your name, by the way.”

Raelyn hesitated a little. The last thing she wanted was someone who knew Jett to see her politicking with a dude she’d just met. *Conversation isn’t cheating though*.

“Raelyn,” she finally said.

A brown-skinned bartender behind the counter approached her and asked what she'd like to drink. Caesar made a gesture to indicate that Rae's bill was on him. Not even a fiancée could stop him from being a gentleman—or going after something he wanted.

The waitress quickly returned with a martini and shot of Hennessey. Raelyn also didn't miss the wink she tossed at Caesar before switching off. *Either she's working hard for a tip or he's quite the ladies' man*, Rae noted. *Either way, I sure as hell wouldn't wanna compete with that. Hell, keeping the birds off Jett is bad enough as is.*

Caesar took a small sip of his drink and continued. "So you supposedly gotta man at home, but yet I keep bumpin' into you in these clubs…"

"What's that supposed to mean?" Rae asked, somewhat offended. She tried her best to downplay it with humor. "My man doesn't have a leash on me," she lied.

Caesar searched Raelyn's eyes as he tried his best to read her. He'd always been a great judge of character. "I find that hard to believe, Raelyn."

Hearing her name roll off his tongue made her instantly weak in the knees. He said it as if they'd known each other a while; almost as if they were familiar with one another.

"Why's that?" Raelyn asked, staring at Caesar a bit too long. She immediately became trapped in his gaze, completely oblivious to her cellphone ringing in her purse.

Caesar scoffed before finishing the rest of his drink. He then turned to face Raelyn who was still patiently waiting on a response.

"Let's get outta here," he said. "This don't even look like yo' type of scene anyway."

Raelyn wouldn't give him the satisfaction of admitting he was right. Instead, she smiled bashfully before turning away. "Look, Caesar, you seem like a cool guy and all…But I told you I have someone."

"Yeah…a nigga that don't gotta leash on you," he reminded her. "Ain't that what you just told me?"

Raelyn didn't respond immediately, so Caesar took it upon himself to lean over and whisper in her ear. "You ain't walk down that aisle yet…" he said. "Fuck with a real nigga, I'll have you second guessin' ole boy. You can believe that."

The hairs on the back of Rae's neck stood erect as his warm breath tickled her skin. Caesar smelled of mint and Clive Christian, and his voice was damn near hypnotic.

"We've been together five years," Raelyn whispered. "And I haven't succumbed to curiosity yet…"

Caesar pulled back and looked deeply into her tight mahogany eyes. "Hell, it ain't nothin' wrong with a lil' curiosity," he told her.

"Not if people get hurt," Raelyn countered.

Caesar didn't respond immediately. Instead, he took his time pulling out his wallet and fetching a crisp bill. Placing a $20 tip on the bar counter, he turned towards Raelyn. "Well, I don't know about all that, ma...But look, I'ma be parked out front for five minutes. I'm in a silver Audi with the top missin'. It's hard not to spot," he told her. "That should give you more than enough time to decide just how *curious* you are."

"And what if I'm not at all?" Raelyn asked.

"Then, hey. That's our loss." And with that, Caesar walked off, leaving Raelyn to her own dangerous thoughts.

Damn him for tempting me, Raelyn thought to herself. She'd never stepped out on Jett before. As a matter of fact, Caesar was the first to ever seriously pique her interest...and it was only day one.

Who said you can't find love in the club?

'Cause I wanna tell them they're wrong...

Come on, just, baby, try a new thing...

And let's spark a new flame...

You gon' be my baby...

Love me, love you crazy...

Tell me if you with it...

Baby, come and get it...

Try a new thing...

And let's spark a new flame...

Chris Brown and Usher cheered Raelyn on as she sat at the bar fighting with her inner demons. *Damn it*! *I am curious*, she finally admitted. Shaking her head, Raelyn couldn't believe Caesar had already left such a lasting impression on her. There had been plenty guys who stepped to Raelyn over the years, but none with the same finesse as Caesar.

Taking a small sip of her drink, Raelyn pulled out her cellphone. Jett had called twice and left some less than tasteful text messages as well. Apparently, he wasn't all too thrilled with her cutting out unexpectedly. As usual, he was treating her as if she were an underage child.

You stay squawking about that wedding that ain't even happened yet, Raelyn heard Symba say.

Slowly, Raelyn looked down at her stolen engagement ring. Dozens of thoughts raced through her mind as she thought about her life and relationship. *Am I settling because I'm content? Or am I content because I'm settling*, she asked herself.

Suddenly, Raelyn's cellphone began ringing again. As expected, it was Jett blowing up her line. Rae didn't even bother responding as she stared down at her phone blankly. Honestly, Jett and his nonsense was the furthest thing from her mind.

Hell, you only live once, a small voice in the back of her mind whispered.

Tossing her iPhone back inside her custom clutch, Raelyn climbed out the bar stool, downed her beverage, and walked off…

EIGHT

"Aye, you see Rae?" Blue asked, looking through the crowd of people from the VIP section on the 2nd floor. "Seems like she should've been back by now."

Just when Symba was about to respond, her phone buzzed indicating an incoming text message. Pulling out her iPhone, she unlocked it and scanned the details—but as soon as Blue walked over, she quickly closed it. The last thing Symba wanted was Blue to see who was hitting her up.

Why the hell am I still out with this broad? It's damn near 2 a.m. I could be at home getting pounded by now, Symba thought.

Blue plopped down on the comfy leather sofa beside her friend. "Did you hear me?" she asked.

"Oh, my fault. Um…No, I ain't seen Rae since she went to the bathroom earlier," Symba responded. She fake scanned the crowd since all of her attention was now on sex. Instead of looking for Raelyn, she was looking for the next orgasm.

Suddenly, as if on cue, an arm draped over her shoulder from behind. "I'm lightweight disappointed to see you blew me off to hang with these clowns," a familiar voice said.

***

Raelyn's Giuseppe heels clicked against the pavement as she walked outside. People were still anxiously waiting in line even though the place was scheduled to close in an hour. *What the hell am I thinking? Am I really gonna do this*, Raelyn asked herself.

Her long, bone straight tresses blew in the wind as she scanned the street for Caesar's car. The moment she spotted his shiny foreign, she knew it was too late to turn back. He'd already called her bluff, and Rae would be lying if she said she wasn't somewhat interested.

"Well, I'll be damned," Caesar said, turning down his music. For a second, he really didn't think Raelyn was going to show—especially since it was nearing that five minute mark. Not only that, but she seemed stuck on her fiancee. He doubted she'd actually give a nigga a chance.

A smile slowly formed on Caesar's face as he switched the gears into drive and pulled up on her. He was glad to see that Raelyn had made the right choice…though he truly felt sorry for her nigga.

***

"Canyon?" Symba asked; surprise etched on her beautiful face.

"Boss, I promise you nobody touched her," one of the guys said, holding his hands up in mock surrender. Sarcasm twinkled in his eyes; he'd been trying to get with Symba since she walked in the VIP.

Boss? Symba thought.

As soon as Canyon entered the section, every fella stood to his feet and showed him love accordingly. *Damn. They acting like this nigga Jeezy or Tip*, Symba noted. Blue looked equally as confused—but impressed nonetheless.

What the women didn't know was that they were looking at a well-respected emperor of a tightly ran organization. Most of the men hanging in the VIP were on Caesar and Canyon's payroll—some of their occupations ranging from street level workers to managers.

"That's good to hear. 'Cuz this one strictly off limits," Canyon said, making himself comfortable next to Symba. He then draped an arm around her shoulder and pulled her close; almost as if he were staking his claim.

"Is that right?" Symba asked with a slight smirk.

"Somethin' like that."

Symba licked her plump lips and stared at Canyon enticingly. “Me and limits don’t coincide,” she told him.

“Well damn. We already got somethin’ in common then,” Canyon smiled.

Feeling like the odd third wheel, Blue pulled out her cellphone and sent a text to the man who’d been on her mind all night.

“Let’s get outta here. I gotta condo not too far—real nice views,” he told her. “Come kick it with me for a hot second. You wastin’ ya time in this mufucka anyway. These niggas in this place ain’t on yo’ level and you know it.”

“How do you know?” Symba challenged.

“’Cuz from the look on ya face, I can tell you ain’t havin’ too much fun,” Canyon said. “Let me be the one to change that…”

Symba didn’t argue when Canyon gently took her hand and helped her to her feet.

“Tell ya girls you’ll get up with them later,” Canyon told her.

Blue waved Symba off as if to say don’t worry about it. She was used to being ditched for some random guy Symba had just met. Instead of taking it personally, Blue realized that’s just how her friend was.

Symba felt odd as she walked hand in hand with Canyon out of the club. It wasn't common for her to be so intimate with a man, especially in public. She was the furthest thing from the girlfriend type. However, Symba did appreciate the envious stares from women she received on the way out.

"You wanna follow me?" Canyon asked, once they were outside in the fresh air.

"I actually rode with my girls. My car is at my friend's place."

"Cool. I'll take you wherever you gotta go in the morning."

"Bet," Symba smiled.

They continued to walk hand in hand until they finally reached his freshly waxed Bugatti. As soon as Symba climbed inside and fastened her seat, her cellphone began ringing.

Oh my God. Why is this nigga blowing me up tonight?

"Excuse me for a second," Symba told Canyon.

He respectively turned down the volume so she could answer her phone.

"What's up?"

"You tell me. You wit' Rae right now?" Jett asked; his voice laced with irritation.

Symba rolled her eyes in annoyance. She hated whenever Jett called her about Raelyn. "No," she said. "I'm not. I'll hit you later—"

"Hol' up," Jett quickly said before she hung up. "What'chu gettin' into tonight? When I'ma see you again?"

"I'll get back to you on that," Symba said before disconnecting the call.

Truthfully, she didn't want talk to Jett with Canyon nearby. Symba already felt bad about creeping with her best friend's man behind her back. But unfortunately, the guilt wasn't strong enough to make her stop. She and Jett had been messing with each other an entire year and they didn't plan on ceasing their affair any time soon.

Jett appreciated Symba for respecting his relationship and keeping shit on the low. Because of how easy she made things for him, he continued coming back. Unlike the other broads Jett smashed from time to time, Symba never got messy. She never threatened to tell Raelyn if he backed off for too long. For Jett, nothing was better than pussy with no strings attached. For Symba it was all about the sex. Nothing more, nothing less.

"One of ya suitors?" Canyon joked, switching the gears to drive. Sarcasm oozed from his tone. He already figured Symba was a hot commodity.

"Not at all," she said, turning up his music.

Curren$y's "*Coupes and Leers*" filled the custom speakers as they cruised through downtown Atlanta.

***

"You know outta all the years I've lived in Atlanta I have never been here before," Raelyn said, taking in her scenery. The two were nestled in a private rooftop setting on top of a 5 star building in Midtown. With sweeping views of the skyline, a crystal Blue pool, elegant fireplaces, and a bar, it was just the type of atmosphere Raelyn liked. All that rowdy shit wasn't really her speed. But over the years she'd learned to adapt since her friends and man loved it.

Other than a second couple who stayed to themselves, Caesar and Raelyn were the only ones there.

A full moon hovered brightly in the dark starry sky. Jazz music played softly in the background. Wispy clouds of smoke sifted through the air as Caesar puffed on a Cohiba Cuban Cigar, and Raelyn a blueberry flavored hookah.

The young couple sat outdoors in a comfy canopy sofa. A bottle of Dom Pérignon Rosé sat in front of them on a round accent table.

"Glad I could show you somethin' new," Caesar smiled, revealing that deep dimpled smile again. *Fuck with me, I'll show you a whole lot more*, he thought to himself. But he wouldn't dare tell her that. First, he had to be sure Raelyn was worth it.

Suddenly, her cellphone vibrated in her purse. Raelyn hadn't even bothered to let her girls know that she was stepping out. Two peas in a pod, Rae figured Blue and Symba could entertain each other for the evening with no problem.

However, much to Raelyn's surprise, it was neither one of her girls. Unfortunately, the caller was none other than Jett harassing her for the hundredth time. Rae's cheeks instantly flushed in embarrassment. Nothing was worse than having your man call while you were somewhere romantic with another.

This is the life I chose though, Raelyn reminded herself.

"You need to get that?" Caesar asked politely after noticing her sudden mood change.

"Um…I…" Rae quickly cleared her throat. "No." With that said she placed her phone on silent and put it back inside her purse.

Caesar, flattered by the gesture, smiled before leaning over to pour them both a generous glass of wine. “So I gotta question for you,” he began. “You ‘bout to be walkin’ down the aisle real soon, right?”

“Yeah,” Rae answered, half-heartedly.

Giving her the side eye, he asked, “Are you *really* ready to spend the rest of yo’ life with ole’ boy? I mean, be real. You duckin’ and dodgin’ dude’s calls now. You sure you ready for forever?”

Raelyn started to eagerly respond with yes, until she carefully mulled over the question. She’d never put so much thought into it until that very moment.

Caesar took it upon himself to ask her a second question since it didn’t seem like she was going to answer the first. “Are you happy?”

Raelyn smiled weakly. “Of course,” she uttered. The response almost felt forced; programmed even.

Caesar gave a flirtatious smile. “Enough that you on a date with me…”

“Woah!” Raelyn laughed. “We just met today. Who said this was a date?”

Caesar chuckled before taking another pull on his cigar. “You right. We chillin’. I shouldn’t get ahead of myself…not with a married woman anyway—”

"*Soon* to be married woman," Raelyn corrected him.

Caesar laughed and then regained his composure quickly. Staring into Rae's eyes, he tried his best to read her. She seemed sweet enough, but he knew there was much more to the surface. "What dude do for a livin?" he asked curiously.

Raelyn almost choked on the wine going down. "Excuse me?"

"Just 'cuz this ain't a date, don't mean I'm not curious about you," Caesar said with a serious expression. "Hell, I wanna know what the competition lookin' like."

Raelyn hesitated. "Jett…he um…He does what he has to do…That's all I can say."

Caesar slowly nodded his head in understanding. "Jett gets his money, huh?" he repeated, sarcasm evident in his voice. "One of *those* types?"

Raelyn's cheeks instantly flushed in embarrassment. Suddenly, she felt as if she were being judged.

"So from the way it sounds, buddy ain't even got a legitimate check." Caesar stared at Raelyn earnestly. He hated to see good women faithful to lame niggas. "You too beautiful to be wastin' ya time on a nigga like that."

Raelyn looked down at the glass of wine in front of her. Once again she stalled with a response. "I should go," she quickly said, standing to her feet.

Caesar gently touched her wrist, before slowly lowering her back down. "Look, my bad, ma. I ain't tryin' to disrespect you. And I apologize if it came off that way," he said. "Have a seat. I ain't ready to let you go just yet..."

Raelyn slowly relaxed a little, but remained silent.

"Look, I'ma just throw it out there," Caesar finally said. "I'm feelin' you. And I wanna get to know more about *you*."

Raelyn shifted nervously in her seat. She was so attracted to Caesar that it was almost unbearable. But the fact still remained the same. She was engaged to Jett.

"What about you?" Rae suddenly asked, switching the focus to Caesar. "I know you've got a lady somewhere—constantly fighting for your love and attention. I saw you with all those groupies earlier."

"It's nice to know you were a checkin' for a nigga," he smiled. "But groupies? Nah," Caesar laughed. "I'ma people's person before anything else, real shit. I treat folks right. That's all. Now as far as an old lady…there isn't one to speak on—*yet*."

"I'm sure there are candidates," Raelyn retorted with a playful grin.

Staring her dead in the eyes, Caesar said, "You'd be first runner up…"

Raelyn quickly looked away in embarrassment. She could feel her cheeks warming up. Rae hadn't been that close to any other man but her own. It almost felt foreign chilling with someone new, even if it was just over drinks and light conversation.

In a low voice, Raelyn spoke, "Caesar, I—"

"Look, you gotta nigga. I understand that. But like I said you ain't walked down the aisle yet. And for a nigga like me, that's still open opportunity," he said. "Hell, while you playin', somethin' new might be just what you need."

NINE

Symba tried her best to keep her mouth from hitting the hardwood floors as she walked through Canyon's impressive penthouse condo. The luxury unit sat high on the 32nd floor. Large glass windows that stretched from the travertine floors to the ceiling boasted breathtaking scenery. There were no buildings and city lights, only the moon surrounded by thin cerulean clouds. It was nostalgic. Peaceful.

"You have a beautiful home," Symba said, trying not to appear awestruck.

"Oh, this? This ain't even the real crib," Canyon bragged. "Just a lil' place I come to and chill every now and then. Lil' getaway spot."

"You mean a place you bring all your freaks to?" Symba teased, pulling off her mini leather jacket.

"Why it gotta be all that?" Canyon laughed.

Symba watched as he walked over to the wet bar and prepared drinks.

"Back at the bar," Symba began. "One of the guys called you boss. What do you do?"

Canyon didn't respond immediately as he headed back over to Symba. She was leaned against a huge window looking out at the night. "You wanna see somethin' dope?" he asked, disregarding her question.

Before Symba could respond, Canyon hit an automatic button on the wall that made the entire barrier of windows slide back. Within seconds, Symba stood on the patio of his penthouse suite. Canyon never missed an opportunity to show off, and oftentimes Caesar lectured him about that. He stressed that being that way could ultimately get them caught up in some shit.

Canyon couldn't help it though. Growing up broke, it felt good to floss what he'd worked so hard for. Besides, the bitches loved it so why would he ever let up?

Symba's eyes widened in shock, clearly impressed. "Impressive..."

Canyon handed her a glass of Moet and stepped over to the balcony. Little did Symba know, she was only the second to ever grace his condo; the first being his baby mama Kaleesi. Fucking with him, most females usually got the "hotel treatment": some dick, a meal in the morning, and a couple hundred if they were truly worth it.

Canyon didn't believe letting women too close—especially after all the drama with Kaleesi…but there was something about Symba…something different.

Symba joined Canyon at the rail and studied his side profile. He was incredibly handsome with his smooth caramel skin, chiseled jawline, and thick lips. His eyes were her true weakness though. They reminded Symba of Autumn leaves, and she wasn't sure but she could've sworn they changed colors. They were definitely green back at the club.

"You never answered me," Symba said. "What do you do for a living?"

Canyon downed his beverage and placed it on the nearby wicker table. He then turned towards Symba and pulled her close. "You ask too many questions," he said. He was close enough for their noses to touch.

Unable to fight the attraction any longer, Symba leaned in to kiss him. "You're right," she whispered.

Canyon's grip around her small waist tightened as they kissed passionately. He was tempted to bend her over the railing, but didn't want to get ahead of himself. "Come on. Let's go inside," he told Symba after pulling apart.

Symba gladly obliged. After all, it was getting a little chilly outside.

After closing up, Canyon turned towards Symba. "Take your shoes off. Get comfortable," he told her, motioning towards an ivory button tufted sectional.

"Well, aren't you quite the host," Symba teased, sashaying towards the sofa. A large silver hand knotted rug rested in the middle of the spacious living room. The pod lighting was turned down low, giving the atmosphere a warm and welcoming feel. The furniture was minimal but nicely put together. Symba was beyond dazzled.

With the push of a remote control button, the huge fire place at the head of the room lit up. Symba took a seat on the cozy sofa and slid off her black Aquazzura lace booties. She then ran her bare toes along the $1100 imported rug.

Canyon slowly turned a dial on a wall. Seconds later R. Kelly's melodic voice filled the built in speakers, playing throughout the condo.

You must be used to me spendin'...

And all that sweet winin and dinin'...

Well I'm fuckin you tonight...'

Symba studied Canyon with seductive eyes as he headed back over to her. All the teasing he was doing was killing her. Yet she could tell from his poise that he loved the anticipation. *I hope his effort's worth it*, Symba thought.

Taking a seat next to her, Canyon passed Symba a tightly rolled blunt. "Aye, let's play a game...," he said from leftfield.

Symba raised a perfectly arched brow in skepticism. "A game? Are you serious?"

Canyon gently took her hand in his and lowered her down onto the rug she seemed to enjoy. "The rules are simple," he began. "If I guess something right about you, you have to remove a piece of clothin'. If I'm wrong, I gotta strip," he told her. "Whoever's the last dressed wins. Loser cooks breakfast in the a.m. You down?"

Symba gently bit down on her bottom lip. She was a freak so she was all about foreplay. Plus, she loved a good competition. "Bet," she finally agreed.

Canyon lifted a wine glass to Symba's mouth and watched as she took a diminutive sip. Afterwards, he sucked the sweet taste of her small tongue. "I'll go first…"

Symba let her hair down and got comfortable. "Shoot."

For several seconds, Canyon simply stared at her in silence. "You ain't ever met a nigga like me…"

Symba smiled before pulling her white mesh shoulder dress over her head. "So far…," she added.

Canyon chuckled before quickly regaining his composure. Getting serious again, he continued with his next guess. "You were a daddy's girl…"

Symba laughed at his statement. "Nuh-uh, nigga. Strip."

"Damn, like that?" Canyon chuckled, pulling off his $300 Pierre Balmain tee.

Symba admired his chiseled, tattooed arms. There was nothing she liked more than a man that took care of his body. "My turn," she said. "*Hmm*…I'm not the first chick you played this game with…"

Canyon reached for the button to his jeans but stopped suddenly. "Nah…Strip…"

"Are you kidding me?" Symba giggled.

"Dead ass," he laughed. "Now come up out that bra…"

Symba shook her head in disbelief. She'd been so sure of her last assumption that she was surprised to find out otherwise. "You'd better be keeping it real," Symba said, reaching for her bra hook. "That's the whole point of the game, right?"

Canyon took a long pull from the blunt and released it through slightly parted lips. "That's all I know how to do, shawty…"

Satisfied with his response, Symba slowly removed her bra, freeing her small perky breasts. Canyon wet his lips after seeing her silver nipple rings. Her chocolate mounds stood erect, and his mouth instantly watered at the sight.

"Your turn," Symba said, bringing him back to reality.

"Okay…let's see…" Canyon rubbed his hands together to prepare for his next guess. "*Umm…*You recently had your heart broken…"

Symba smiled and slowly shook her head. "Strip," she instructed.

Canyon sucked his teeth before sliding out of his A.P.C. jeans. "Aight…you got that one," he said.

Symba took another sip of her wine as she studied him for several seconds. "You date multiple women at once…"

Canyon looked at her pointedly before removing his crisp wife beater. Symba's dark eyes anxiously scanned his buff torso before settling on the dime-sized scar on his abdomen. Her curiosity about him instantly grew threefold.

"…You live a dangerous life," Symba whispered.

Keeping his gaze locked on hers, Canyon pulled off his thin black socks. Symba was immediately impressed by the fact that he had nice feet. They even looked as if he kept them well-maintained.

Symba was so turned on by the sight of Canyon in nothing but his boxers that she could barely think straight.

"Um…let me see…," she said, searching for her next guess.

Without warning, Canyon crawled over to Symba and climbed on top. "I forfeit," he whispered before leaning down to kiss her.

"So you cookin' me breakfast in the a.m.?" Symba smiled.

"Fasho…"

The bright lights from the fireplace reflected off Canyon, making him look sexier than ever. Suddenly, an unfamiliar feeling washed over Symba. One that was indescribable; something she'd never felt.

"I'm sorry but I gotta go," Symba said, pushing him off.

Canyon looked up at her, completely confused. His dick was so big and hard that she could see his mushroom shaped head peeking out the end of his boxers.

Have mercy, Symba thought, grabbing up her clothes. Truth be told, she was scared what sex would do to her afterward. The last thing she wanted was to get caught up. *I love Raelyn but I ain't trying to end up like that bitch*, Symba told herself.

"Why are you leaving?" Canyon asked from the floor.

"I just realized some shit I gotta do. I'll call you in the morning," Symba rambled off, racing towards the door.

Before Canyon could ask how she was getting home, he heard the front door slam shut.

Symba didn't stop walking until she reached the nearest cab at the end of the block. After hopping in the backseat, she pulled out her cell and searched through various booty call numbers. Tonight, Jett was out of the question so she settled on a new guy she'd meet two weeks ago at the post office. Unlike Canyon she knew what to expect with him.

Damn Canyon for getting me so worked up, Symba thought. *Now I gotta have another nigga finish what he started.*

Symba laughed at herself when she realized how crazy she must've looked to Canyon running out. *I gotta stay away from that man*, she told herself.

TEN

Blue tapped lightly on room 1502's door and waited patiently for a response. After several seconds, the door slowly creaked open. Zac stood on the opposite end, using the door as a shield to cover his bruised face. After tonight, he found out just how much love could hurt.

"Can I come in?" Blue whispered.

Zac grimaced, his jaw tightening as he pondered on the decision. He'd received several texts from Blue after the fiasco took place; none of which he'd responded to. After the way she played him back at her crib, he wasn't really feeling her at the moment. Zac's father had warned him about females like Blue at an early age…but those were the types he usually went for. Loud-mouthed chicks with attitude problems, good pussy, and their share of baggage. *Find a good woman with a degree and no drama*, Zachariah Sr. preached. But Zac wasn't trying to hear all that. He knew what he wanted…and that was Blue.

Without a word, Zac stepped to the side and allowed her entrance. For the last two weeks, he'd been residing inside a five star Mandarin-Oriental suite. Initially there for business, Zac somehow fell off track trying to chase after Blue. She always had that effect on him, and he was helpless to it.

Born to a wealthy real-estate developer, Zac had been spoiled with a lavish life since birth. He attended private schools all up until he graduated and went off to Florida A&M University.

After obtaining his bachelor's degree, Zac officially joined his father's company. With no children, he had a six-figure income job, pushed a 2014 Rolls Royce Phantom, and yet and still insisted on chasing after a chick with a man. Whenever Zac fell, he fell hard. Unfortunately, his big heart was his weakness—and Blue knew it.

Feeling bad for everything that happened earlier, she slowly walked up to Zac and reached for his face. He unexpectedly moved from her reach and walked over towards the cream chaise. Taking a seat, Zac looked up at Blue and patiently waited for an explanation. After realizing he wasn't going to get one, he spoke first. "What are you here for, Blue?"

"Look, I'm sorry about that shit with Deon," Blue finally said. "But nobody told you to pop uninvited. I mean, what were you thinking?"

"I was thinkin' you'd finally come to your senses and realize when you got a good thing," Zac responded. "But I guess I was delusional, huh? Just kiddin' myself like I been doin' since day one—"

"Zac—"

"Why are you here...*seriously*?"

Blue could clearly see the pain and irritation etched on Zac's handsome face. He was so weak for her and she knew it. Suddenly, Blue felt badly for the way things played out that evening. At that moment, all she wanted to do was make everything right.

Keeping her gaze locked on his, Blue tossed her clutch on the king size bed and slowly undressed. Zac remained silent as he watched every article of clothing hit the plush chocolate carpet. His dick instantly sprang to life at the sight of her naked petit frame. Blue was built like a goddess with curves that most women envied or paid for. The tattoos covering most of her body only added to her sexiness.

"I'm here 'cuz I wanna be yours for the night…," Blue whispered, slowly approaching him.

Zac slowly stood to his feet, towering over Blue by an entire foot. "That's the thing, Blue…I don't just want you for the night…," he admitted. "And if that's the best, you got to give, I'm straight. I'm tired of playin' games."

"Your mouth sayin' one thing but *this* saying another." Blue gave his erection a gentle squeeze, and Zac released a breath in response. She had him harder than a Calculus test. Without warning, Blue lowered herself to his waist level and unfastened his dark khaki Chinos.

Running his fingers through her long, wavy hair, Zac admired the sight of Blue from his position. In silent anticipation, he watched as she took half his ten-inch dick in her mouth. "Damn…," he moaned, gripping her hair tighter. Slowly, he guided her head up and down his impressive length. Blue's epic head game was one-third of the reason he was pussy whipped in the first place.

When Zac could no longer stand the foreplay, he helped Blue to her feet and lifted her in his arms. Carrying her to the bed, he play tossed her on the mattress and pulled his shirt off. Zac didn't have one tattoo on his perfect body, and for Blue that was also a turn on.

After pulling off his Bulgari prescription glasses, Zac placed them on the nightstand and began pulling his pants down.

Blue bit her bottom lip seductively as she played with her pierced clit. Whenever Zac took his glasses off before sex, he turned from Bruce Banner into the Incredible Hulk. He switched egos the minute his dick grew. Seemingly, a good guy to everyone else, Zac was an absolute animal in the bedroom.

Latching onto a smooth vanilla leg, he yanked her down towards the edge of the bed and flipped her over onto her stomach. "Put that ass up like I like it," he instructed.

Blue eagerly did as she was told, arching her back and tooting her round booty in the air. Zac despised the sight of Deon's name written in bold cursive across her right cheek. But as usual, he covered it with his large hand before sliding inside her sopping kitty.

"*Ooooh*, damn, Zac! Fuck me," Blue whimpered, trying her best to throw it back.

Zac's curved pole stroked her spot repeatedly with each powerful thrust. Cream lathered his massive dick as she grew wetter by the second. Not even Deon could hit it like Zac. And honestly, that was the best part of it all to her. Whenever Blue and Zac had sex, he pounded her like he was trying to out-fuck Deon.

"Oh, shit! You 'bout to make me cum!" Blue moaned, gripping the nearby sheets.

Zac quickly slipped out of her and flipped her over onto her back. "I ain't tell you you can come yet," he said, mounting her.

Blue acrobatically pulled her legs back behind her head so that her pussy was open access. Gripping her soft, plump ass, Zac guided himself inside her wet chamber. Her kitty was so tight around his thick pipe, that it snatched his dick back with every stroke. "Fuck, Blue. This pussy so good," he whispered. "You wonder why a mufucka don't wanna share. You know what'chu got."

"Damn…I love you!" Blue bellowed in the midst of ecstasy.

Zac quickly sped up his pace. He was used to her talking shit whenever he hit it right, so he paid her words no mind. After all, when it was all said and done, he planned on making her fall equally as hard.

"Shit, I'm 'bout to cum!" Blue hollered, tightening her muscles around his dick.

"Come on. Come with me," Zac urged before kissing her passionately.

Blue's toes instantly curled as her body quaked with an orgasm so powerful it sent her eyes rolling to the back of her head.

Seconds later, Zac snatched his glistening dick free and stroked it until he skeeted his cum over Blue's c-cup breasts. Once he was empty, he collapsed next to Blue who was still struggling to catch her breath.

I don't know how much longer I can juggle two men, she thought.

ELEVEN

Jett awoke the following day with sunlight streaming onto his face and Raelyn on his right. He was tempted to shake her ass up out her sleep and demand where she was last night, but decided against it. Besides, he didn't have the energy thanks to a hangover. After his football team's victory, Jett, Roman, and Ace went out and turned up.

They met a couple chicks at Havana in Buckhead, and Jett enjoyed himself with two at a nearby motel. He'd gotten so fucked up last night, he didn't realize he'd drove home and fallen asleep with a used condom on his dick. Needless to say, Jett was surprised to discover his flaccid dick inside a cum-filled Trojan that morning.

Damn. You slippin' bruh, Jett thought to himself. He was grateful, Raelyn hadn't noticed it.

Climbing out his king size bed, Jett padded barefoot to the adjoined bathroom. Tossing the condom in the toilet, he proceeded with his morning piss and shit. Afterwards, he hopped in the shower before brushing his teeth and flossing.

When Jett returned to the bedroom, Raelyn was wide awake, sitting up in bed with her knees drawn to her chest. "You heading out?" she asked curiously.

"Yeah," Jett answered, dabbing on a bit of designer cologne. "So where you crept yo' ass out to yesterday?" he asked, finally turning to face Raelyn. She was the only woman who woke up flawless. Even without makeup she was remarkable.

Although Jett and Raelyn had their ups and downs, he loved her more than he loved himself. Rae was the first chick he'd ever loved, and there wasn't a bitch alive that could compete. Though he smashed many on the regular, none was worth labeling wifey. Raelyn had long earned her title.

"I…uh…" Rae cleared her throat like she usually did whenever she was nervous. "Blue and Deon got into it again. She needed me to come and deescalate things."

Jett sighed in disappointment. He got irritated whenever he heard Rae's ratchet ass friends' names. "What I tell you about runnin' with them hoes?"

Raelyn felt like a child being scolded by her father. "She needed me…"

Jett pulled on a pair of jeans and took a seat on the bed beside Rae. "Them hoes ain't nothin' but wolves in sheeps' clothin'."

Raelyn looked down in silence. She could've said the same thing about him. Rae hated whenever Jett talked down on her girls. After all, it wasn't like she particularly cared about his friends.

"I guess…" she murmured.

Jett slowly stood to his feet and walked towards the huge walk in closet. Half of it was filled with his shoes; he loved kicks like a teenage girl loved Justin Bieber.

As soon as Jett disappeared inside, Rae's cellphone buzzed on the nightstand, indicating a text message. Reaching over, she grabbed it and unlocked it. *Caesar*.

A small smile formed across her lips as she reminisced on their evening. After drinks on the rooftop deck, Caesar treated them to Greek omelets at the Metro Café Diner on Peachtree. Truthfully, Rae didn't want their night to end. Caesar had great conversation, he was a gentleman, and he made sure she got home safely without trying any funny business.

Look at yourself. Getting caught up already, Raelyn said to herself.

She started to ignore the message, but once again curiosity got the best of her. After unlocking her phone, she opened the text from Caesar.

Raelyn was surprised to see an address attached to the words: *Good morning beautiful. Meet me here in 2 hours. I'll be patiently waiting…*

The moment Jett walked back in the bedroom, Raelyn quickly exited the message and placed her phone down.

"Aye, bay. Which kicks should I wear?" Jett asked, holding up two pairs of multicolored Nikes. Long black and green pot leaf socks covered his legs; he was dressed just like he was about to get into some shit.

"Um…I guess the ones on the left," Raelyn said only half-interested.

As usual, Jett settled on the pair she didn't choose. "Go get ya hair done or buy yaself somethin' nice," he said, tossing her a small wad of cash. Jett always gave her a little something-something whenever he was getting ready to hit a lick, so Rae already knew what time it was.

"Thanks…Love you," Raelyn told him.

"I know you do," Jett said before walking out.

As soon as Raelyn heard the front door close shut, she quickly hopped out the bed, and rushed to get ready. She had her own trouble she planned on getting into…and it involved Caesar…

TWELVE

It was fifteen minutes past noon when Symba finally rolled over, yawned, and stretched in bed. She nearly jumped out her skin at the sight of the unrecognizable naked man next to her. She hardly even remembered having company last night—let alone a one night stand.

Shaking her head, Symba chuckled lightly to herself. She went through dicks like a teenager went through relationships. It was to the point where every face was a blur. Every touch, every kiss was forgotten. Hell, the orgasms were barely memorable…and it was because of that Symba's hunger for sex was insatiable.

"*Mmm,*" the strange man moaned before turning over to stretch. "Mornin', beautiful."

Disgusted by the fact that he'd overstayed his welcome, she rolled her eyes, climbed out the bed, and sashayed into her master bathroom. *I hope he takes the damn hint and leaves,* Symba thought. Most fellas rolled out after busting their nuts. Why the hell did he think it was okay to stay the night?

Pulling her panties down her legs, Symba plopped down on her heated toilet seat and tinkled. Just as she was getting comfortable in the privacy of the room, last night's fling barged inside the bathroom.

"Oh, I'm sorry," he said, preparing to leave—but suddenly changing his mind in mid-step. "Um…actually, I was just wondering if you were hungry. If so, we could grab a bite to eat at the Waffle House on—"

"Look…" Symba cut him off. "I'm sorry—what was your name again?"

"Spencer," he answered. The confused look on his face questioned how she could even forget after the passionate night they shared.

"Spencer," Symba continued. "You seem like a great guy and all…but I don't do the whole *routine* thing."

"Excuse me?"

Symba lit a Newport and took a light pull. "You know…the whole we meet, we fuck, we date, we break…"

Spencer chuckled at her unexpected response. "Are you serious?"

"Dead ass. I seriously don't wanna waste your time," Symba told him. "Now if you don't mind…I'd like a little privacy."

Spencer looked at Symba like she'd just sprouted a third eye. "Like that?" he asked, clearly offended.

"Lock up behind you," Symba said unenthused.

Shaking his head in disappointment, Spencer backpedaled out of the bathroom, and quietly let himself out.

Good riddance.

Symba relaxed a little when she finally heard the front door close behind him. That was just the way she liked shit; simple.

Symba had just begun preparing a hot breakfast when her cellphone suddenly rang. A part of her feared it was the John Doe who'd angrily left her house moments ago. Needless to say, she was somewhat surprised to see Canyon's name flashing across the screen. After the way she'd run out on him last night, she didn't expect a call so soon.

"Hello?" Symba answered.

"Hey. I'm not catching you at a bad time, am I?" It sounded like he was driving on his end.

Symba placed an unopened pack of turkey bacon on the kitchen counter. "Not really," she said. "What's up?"

Canyon chuckled lightly. "You tell me," he said.

"Canyon, about last night—"

"Look, it really don't even matter," he told her. "I got a lil' free time right now and was wonderin' if you wanted to grab a bite. I could come and swoop you up in twenty."

What the hell about today has all these men wanting to feed me, Symba asked herself. She even wondered if she looked slimmer than usual. One hundred thirty-five pounds soaking wet, Symba had always been a slender woman but she made up for it with her statuesque height and fat ass.

Symba pondered over his offer for a few seconds. She'd just told the last nigga that she was cool…but something about Canyon made her want to say yes.

"I'll text you my address," Symba said before disconnecting the call.

A small smile spread across her face. Something told her Canyon was going to give her a run for her money.

***

Raelyn's knee high Tom ford heels clicked against the wooden planks as she walked over to Caesar. He stood at the edge of the dock near a beautiful yacht resting on Lake Allatoona. *Had I would've known we were meeting here, I would've worn something more comfortable*, she thought.

Raelyn looked immaculate that afternoon in a cream Chanel tunic. Her hair was down, and Gucci sunglasses covered her mint-colored eyes.

"Such an atypical place to meet," Raelyn said after reaching him.

Caesar turned towards her and smiled. Her style was on point; she didn't cease to impress him. "I just got it this morning," he said, turning back to face the yacht.

Caesar had spent well over two hundred thousand dollars on the luxury Marquis yacht. A three tier vessel, it offered three separate decks, a dining area, full bar, and state of the art kitchen. It was the perfect escape from the city life—which even he needed a break from every now and then.

"Got a great deal on it too," he lied, in an attempt to be modest. "Hey, you hungry?"

"Starving," Raelyn said. She'd only eaten a Nutri-Grain bar on the way out before embarking on the 45-minute drive.

Caesar offered his hand for her to take so he could help her onto the yacht. Raelyn carefully climbed on board, taking in the breathtaking scenery of the wooded area. Sunlight reflected off the bluish green waters, offering a rustic feel. It was absolutely beautiful. Raelyn only hoped Caesar wasn't dangerous.

Stop thinking so foolishly, her conscious scolded.

"This is beautiful, Caesar," Raelyn told him. "I don't think I've ever been on a yacht before."

Caesar kept his hold on her hand as he led her to the cockpit. "I hope you like seafood," he said.

"I love it," Raelyn smiled.

Her eyes instantly shot open in surprise at the sight of a dining table adorned in various seafood dishes and platters. Freshly caught lobsters, crab legs, oysters, crawfish, and a plethora of shrimp awaited their arrival.

"Oh my God. You did all this?" Raelyn asked.

Caesar guffawed. "I hired a lil' help," he said.

"This looks great," Raelyn told him, sliding in the booth.

Everything around them was so quiet and peaceful—especially since they were all alone. Raelyn could hear every bird and insect's chirp, and she absolutely loved it. She'd always been the outdoor type.

"Glad to see you could get away for a lil' while to enjoy this with me," he said.

Raelyn's cheeks flushed after Jett came to mind. He'd have a fit if he knew she was kicking it with someone new.

***

Weed permeated the air surrounding Jett, Ace, and Roman. As usual, they were hot as hell with drugs in their system and an assortment of weapons in the trunk. However, that was the life of a young, reckless nigga—and Jett was the definition of that.

If that wasn't bad enough, they were driving around Atlanta in a police cruiser replica. They'd been tailing a white 2011 Mercedes-Benz Sprinter van for the last ten minutes. As dirty as it was, that was one of the many ways they made their paper. When the trio weren't running up in houses, they were intervening drug transportations. And unfortunately, Demarcus White was their chosen target.

A mousy brown-skinned guy in his mid-twenties, Demarcus gained his position after meeting Canyon in jail. Back in his younger and reckless days, he'd served a little time with the young boss who promised to look out for him when he got out.

That was Canyon though. He was a humble dude quick to help the next nigga make a dollar with his multimillion dollar operation. Caesar, on the other hand, liked to stick his Day-1's. He didn't trust a lot of motherfuckers, and for probable cause. With the money and moves they were making, he could only afford to deal with niggas he truly rocked with.

Demarcus was completely unaware of the vehicle following him as he navigated the van. It was completely wrapped in a legitimate plumbing company's banner so as to keep suspicions down. Canyon had brought out the company a couple years back to launder his drug money through. And with the utility vans, he used them to transport dope.

Usually, Demarcus was always privy to his surroundings, but lately he'd gotten lax. He was doing the one thing Canyon warned him never to do. Demarcus thought he was untouchable, but that day he was about to find out otherwise.

Unbeknownst to him, Jett and his boys had been watching his routine for the last few weeks. They'd also even learned Demarcus' drop off point; a private highly secured mansion tucked in a quiet Druid Hills community. But that was another job in itself. One that they honestly weren't equipped for.

Instead, they decided to pick off of a driver and take the work for themselves. If dude was really holding, Jett could net a serious profit after distribution. He even had a few teenage boys who pushed his stolen product on the streets for the low. With the risky shit they were doing they needed to keep their hands clean at all costs. For years, their hustle had been foolproof.

"Aye, slow down, cuz," Roman said, eyeballing a big booty chick walking her miniature schnauzer.

Ace didn't look impressed in the least. As a matter of fact, there wasn't a bitch in sight who could make him look twice—except for Raelyn. Secretly, he'd been digging her for some time now but the fact that she was his boy's girl was more than enough to keep him at bay. For now.

At times, Ace even found himself tempted to put hands on Jett for the way he treated Raelyn but he knew it wasn't his place. Besides, it wasn't like Rae didn't know what she was getting herself into. She'd had more than enough time to dissect her relationship and realize how fucked up Jett was but she never left. Still, that didn't stop Ace from fantasizing about his homeboy's fiancée.

"Man, fuck dat bitch," Jett said. "We got business to handle. No play time 'til we put in that work, feel me?"

Roman sucked his teeth and slumped back in his seat. At only nineteen, he was the baby of the trio. He'd been running the streets since he was in the second grade, and always stayed in some type of shit.

Roman met Jett when he was fifteen after Jett broke up a brawl between him and another younger boy. Jett always told Roman he reminded him of himself. He quickly took the feisty teenager under his wing and groomed him to be the thug he was today.

Ace, on the hand, had been friends with Jett since they were grabbing asses and running off together. Growing up in east Atlanta, the two had been through everything, and were thick as thieves.

As soon as the van neared a bridgein the historic district, Jett switched on the sirens. Luckily, traffic was sparse that afternoon, and they were the only two vehicles presently on the road.

Jett grinned wickedly as he pulled up behind the van. "Yeah…got his ass," he said. "Aight, get ready…" All at once, they snatched on ski masks and grabbed their heat. They'd been watching and waiting for days, but now it was finally time to put in work.

Meanwhile in the crew van, Demarcus reluctantly put his gears in park. Bright blue and red sirens flashed behind him, lighting up the dark passage. In all the years he'd been delivering, Demarcus had never gotten pulled over by the law. In his mind, he was way too careful. *This can't be life right now*, he thought.

"You gotta be fuckin' kiddin' me, man..."

Demarcus looked back at the unmarked police vehicle in the side view mirror and frowned. The windows were tinted so dark he barely could see the silhouettes behind them.

Suspicions on high alert, Demarcus grabbed his cellphone and prepared to call his boss. He was just about to grab his tool too when the driver's window suddenly exploded in glass.

KSSSSSHHHHHH!

Demarcus' hands' instantly flew up to protect his face and eyes. Tiny, sharp bits and pieces nicked his skin as it littered the seats and floors of the van.

Ace immediately struck Demarcus with the sawed off shotgun after busting out the window. He needed dude to know he wasn't fucking around.

Acting fast, Roman snatched the keys out the ignition and opened the door. Jett roughly yanked Demarcus' out before slamming his ass against the van.

"Nigga, you know what time it is! Where the mufuckin' work?!" Jett demanded, pointing his machine gun pistol in the man's face. If he squeezed, there was no way in hell Demarcus would have an open casket funeral.

"Man, I don't know what the fuck you talkin' 'bout—"

WHAP!

Ace slammed the butt of his gun in Demarcus' nose, instantly shattering the bridge. Dark red blood gushed down his mouth and chin before painting his expensive tee.

"Ah, shit!" Demarcus reached for his broken nose, accidentally dropping his cellphone in the process. He'd never felt anything more excruciating in his life. Yet he knew his problems would only get worse if they located the dope.

"Toss me da keys, cuz. I'm done with his clown ass nigga, I'll find the shit myself," Jett said, heading towards the back of the van.

Demarcus quickly tried to go after him, but Roman stopped him with a fierce punch to the gut. Just for the hell of it, Ace got in a few good licks as well.

While Ace and Roman worked over Demarcus, Jett helped himself to opening the back doors and inspecting its contents. From the looks of things, all seemed well and legitimate. Plumbing equipment and cleaning solutions covered the floor, and Jett almost chucked it up as a bust—until he noticed a faint separation in the carpeting.

Bingo.

Jett eagerly peeled the thin gray material back, revealing multiple bricks of pure uncut cocaine. A slow grin spread across his face, revealing his gold fangs. "Jackpot."

THIRTEEN

Not even ten minutes into their lunch date, Caesar's business phone began ringing. He'd contemplated leaving it in his car, but decided against it. *Damn, this shit better be important*, he thought.

"Excuse me for a second," Caesar said, wiping his mouth. He then pulled out a cheap Motorola and stood to his feet.

Raelyn quickly took note of the iPhone still sitting on the table. *Why does he have two phones*, she asked herself.

"This should only be a minute."

"You're fine," Raelyn smiled.

Excusing himself, Caesar descended the spiral stairs until he was on the second tier. Once he was sure he had enough privacy, he finally flipped open the phone. "What's up, D? Why you hittin' me on this line?" he asked. The disposable minute phone was strictly for emergency business calls only.

Caesar didn't believe in communicating much over traceable lines. He'd seen one too many of his predecessors fall prey to the Feds tapping in. Caesar wanted no parts of it, so he made sure to always have a clean social footprint. *Motherfuckers won't ever catch me slippin'.*

"Boss, I got bad news," Demarcus said through swollen lips. His face was so busted up that his voice came out muffled. He hadn't left the spot under the bridge where he'd been robbed, and honestly, he had no clue what to do next. He'd been working for Caesar and Canyon five years and had never been hit before.

"I don't like the sound of that," Caesar simply said.

"Some niggas in a black squad car pulled up on me not too long ago…"

Caesar's jaw tightened as he listened closely. He already wasn't feeling the direction of the conversation.

"Yo', straight up, I thought the mothafuckas was twelve, man. I pulled over and next thing I know these niggas blam my ass."

"They get the work?" Caesar asked in a serious tone. That was all the information he really cared to know.

Demarcus sighed in disappointment, too ashamed to admit he'd fucked up. "They got all that shit, bruh."

Caesar released a deep breath, but tried his best to remain calm. After all, he had company. "Stay where you are. I'm on my way."

"Yes sir," Demarcus said.

Caesar disconnected the call and drew in a deep breath. It took everything in him to keep from exploding. The last thing he wanted to hear was that he'd lost over half a million dollars' worth of dope.

After regaining his composure, Caesar headed back upstairs to the cockpit. He found Raelyn looking out at the scenery, her long hair blowing in the soft breeze. She was picture perfect.

"I hate to do this, ma, but I'm afraid I gotta cut lunch short," he said. "Some shit just came up and I gotta take care of it ASAP."

"Oh no," Raelyn said. "Well, I hope everything's okay."

"It will be soon," he said, grabbing his car keys and cellphone off the table.

Raelyn climbed out the booth and allowed him to help her exit the vessel. She was sad that their rendezvous had to end so early. But truthfully it was probably for the best. Deep down, Rae knew she had no business chopping it up with another guy anyway.

Although he had an important situation to tend to, Caesar still walked Raelyn to her car and hugged her tightly before she climbed inside. After promising to make up for his prompt departure, Caesar bid Raelyn farewell and headed to his car. Once inside, he called up Canyon.

***

The Presidential was a moniker given to the $1.2 million dollar upscale mansion in Druid Hills, Atlanta. No one resided there, and it had been purchased merely to stash large quantities cocaine.

It was also where Caesar and Canyon held their meetings. Because the private property was nestled deep in the neighborhood, no one ever questioned the many vehicles coming and going at all hours of the day.

A variety of expensive cars sat outside The Presidential. Every local employee from every rank was there to discuss the robbery that had taken place two hours earlier. Caesar and Canyon had been running shit for a while with minimal problems. They'd even built alliances with competitors to make it so everyone could eat fair. It was rare for one of their workers to get jacked. And because of that, the bosses had to call a sit down.

Standing at the head of the room, Caesar stared at the many faces gazing at him. He tried his best to spot disloyalty, but the task was damn near impossible. Every fella—and female—amongst him was a loyal individual he trusted with his life.

"First I wanna know who these niggas are," Canyon said. "Then I wanna know how they knew where and when to hit us." The look of frustration on his face matched Caesar's. He wasn't all too pleased with ending his afternoon early with Symba. Unlike his business partner, Canyon was less rash. Before it was all said done, blood would be shed.

"Ya boy, Demarcus prolly knew the niggas," Lamont, one of the organization's managers spoke up. He was leaned against a wall with a grimace on his chocolate face. He'd never trusted Demarcus so he couldn't wait for an opportunity to throw him under the bus. Like his predecessor, Caesar, he didn't believe in fucking with cats who weren't his Day-1's. Nowadays niggas couldn't be trusted—especially with undercover Feds running rampant.

"Aye, fuck you man!" Demarcus spat through swollen lips. "You think I'd let some niggas do this to me on purpose?" he asked, pointing to his busted up face. He looked as if he'd gotten in a brawl with Floyd Mayweather Jr.

"Man, niggas will do whateva for that check."

"Enough," Canyon spoke up in irritation. "Arguin' ain't gettin' us closer to fixin' shit."

"Yes sir," Demarcus and Lamont said in unison.

Every employee remained silent as they waited for their boss to continue. They all held a high level of respect for Caesar and Canyon. They paid them well and ensured that their families were well taken care of. Everyone's children attended private schools and no one lived in a house under $400,000. All the organization emperors asked in return was loyalty and honesty.

"I want everybody to keep ya eyes open for competitors," Canyon said. "If they peddlin' our shit, we gon' hear about it. And as always, keep ya ears to the streets."

As Canyon spoke, one of his workers relayed the message to the organization's deaf enforcer, June. At only twenty-eight, he stood at a massive 6"9 and was rather burly in stature. Though he didn't speak or hear, he was known in the hood as being able to crush a man's skull with his bare hands.

Due to a troubled life, everyone he knew had outcast him—but not Canyon and Caesar. They happily welcomed June into their organization with open arms and gave him the position of muscle. He and his little brother, Terry had been loyal to their camp for over three years.

"I want everybody to keep ya shit clean. Be twice as alert," Canyon continued. "And if some shit unearths regardin' the niggas who hit us, be sure to speak up. We gon' get dem mufuckas. Believe that."

Every soldier in the room murmured in agreement. There was nothing better than justice being served accordingly.

"What about me?" Demarcus spoke up.

He desperately needed a hospital, but his position was the only thing that mattered to him at the moment. The money he earned as a delivery driver was all he had. A repeat offender, Demarcus doubted any place would hire a felon.

Canyon cut his eyes at the careless employee. “Did you happen to see these niggas’ faces? Could you point ‘em out to me if you had to?” He already knew the answer before it fell from Demarcus’ bloodied lips.

“Nah. They had on masks.”

Canyon tossed his hands up. “Great. Not only are you irresponsible, you also useless.” Fed up with Demarcus, he looked over at June and said, “Get this nigga out my sight. Matter fact, take care his ass for me.”

“Aye, man, what the fuck?!” Demarcus screamed, jumping out his seat. He tried to run, but June was much faster than he looked. Grabbing the tiny guy, he hemmed him up and carried him out the room roughly. His younger brother Terry quickly followed suit. One didn’t move without the other.

“Come on, Canyon! Bruh, I ain’t have shit to do with that lick!” Demarcus yelled.

His pleas sent chills through Canyon, but he had to be firm. Where he was from, treason didn’t go unpunished.

"*CAESAR*!" Demarcus cried in desperation. He continued to thrash about in June's massive arms.

The giant stopped for a split second and looked over at his boss to see what he wanted to do. Without a word, Caesar looked down and walked out of the meeting room. He didn't have shit to say about the situation. Canyon had already made up his mind to have the kid dealt with.

"This meeting's adjourned. Everybody can get back to the money," Canyon said with finality.

"THIS IS SOME BULLSHIT AND YA'LL KNOW IT!" Demarcus screamed on the way out. Sadly, he'd have to pay for his mistake with his life.

Every soldier stood to his feet and shuffled out the room in silence. After today, they knew they'd have to be on their shit if they didn't want to end up like their boy. Canyon didn't fuck around when it came to his money. He'd go from 0 to 100 really quickly, and they all knew it now.

Canyon found Caesar standing in the back of the house, smoking a cigar. He appeared to be in deep thought as he stared out at the beautiful plants, trees, and shrubbery. He paid good money to keep the place well-maintained—even with no one living there.

"You good, bro?" Canyon asked with concern in his tone.

Caesar sighed before releasing a thin cloud of smoke. Keeping his back turned to Canyon he said, "A wise man once told me 'if you want one year of prosperity, grow grain. For ten years of prosperity, grow trees. And for a hundred years, grow people." Caesar then looked over at Canyon. "Bruh, we can't afford to be cuttin' our soldiers loose. Demarcus was a good dude. We need niggas like that on the team."

Canyon paused as he mulled over his response. "Man, dude was like fam, real talk…Shit, I'm da one that put him on. But we in the big leagues now, dawg," he said. "We ain't in Brooklyn no mo' makin' pennies, wishin' we could be the niggas callin' shots. This shit is all we got. Our blood, sweat, and tears. We done put our all into this, bruh. So with that said, what we *can't afford* is mistakes."

Caesar puffed on his cigar. His heart was a lot bigger than Canyon's, but he understood where his brother was coming from. "I agree…" He had no problem bowing down. After all, Canyon was speaking real shit.

Slowly walking over to Caesar, Canyon clapped a hand on his broad back. "Anyway, I saw yo' ass gettin' real cozy with that redbone back at the club yesterday. What's up with that one?"

Caesar chuckled as his mind wandered to Raelyn. "Aw, man. Shit, I'm still tryin' to figure it out myself." He didn't want to tell him she had a man already.

Canyon laughed. “Dig that. Hell, just take it one day at a time.”

“That’s all we can do,” Caesar said.

***

The sun was just beginning to set when Raelyn returned home for the evening. Instead of being piled up in the living room, talking shit and doing drugs, Rae found Jett and his boys at the mirrored dining table. Cocaine bricks and a large scale sat on the surface.

Raelyn’s eyes widened in shock; she’d never seen so much powder at once. From the looks of things, this was one of Jett’s biggest hits.

“Aye, bay. Can you grab me the zip loc bags from the kitchen?” he asked over his shoulder.

Placing her clutch and phone on the marble island, Raelyn fetched the container and went to the dining area. After she placed it on the table, Jett leaned up for a kiss. Ace automatically looked down and continued sorting dope so he wouldn’t have to see it. Roman didn’t miss the awkward gesture, but he refused to speak on it.

Raelyn was just about to head to the bedroom when Jett unexpectedly grabbed her wrist.

Pulling her down towards him, he took a whiff of her clothing. "You smell like cologne…"

FOURTEEN

Ace and Roman's eyes instantly shot to Raelyn as they waited for a response.

Her heart sank to the pit of her stomach as she tried to think of a decent lie. "I…uh…must've dabbed some of yours on by mistake," was the best she could come up with.

Jett gave Raelyn the side eye in suspicion. *Nah, this bitch ain't crazy*, he thought. *Is she*? Jett was just to say something when Ace suddenly caught him off.

"So you know our boy, Raekwon got knocked by Feds a few days ago," he said, coming to Raelyn's defense. "We'll need somebody to take over his block."

Raekwon was a seventeen-year old boy, struggling to pay for college. He attended GSU and sold to the local students while enrolled. Having someone take over his share of work wasn't an issue. Jett was more concerned about Raekwon talking.

"I'll get on that," Jett said, dispassionately.

Taking that as her cue to leave, Raelyn crept off to the bedroom. Once inside, she closed the door, pressed her back against it, and released a sigh of relief. *Caesar's cologne must've stuck to me when we hugged*, Rae thought.

As crazy as it sounded, she couldn't shake the mysterious Caesar from her mind. It'd only been two days, but somehow he managed to conquer her thoughts—and more recently her dreams. Earlier that day, in the shower, Raelyn even found herself comparing her new *friend* to her fiancee. Who had the most appeal, shit like that.

"What the hell are you doing, girl?" Raelyn asked herself. She didn't know Caesar from a can of paint, and that meant she had no idea what was behind his motives.

What's he really trying to get out of it all, Rae wondered. She was sure Caesar had more than enough women to keep him entertained. What could he possibly want with her?

Damn, I have to be more careful.

Raelyn quickly blushed. *Listen to me. Be more careful. What I need to do is stop this before it gets too out of hand.*

Suddenly, Raelyn's cellphone buzzed indicating a text message. Tucking her hair behind her ear, she pulled out her iPhone and unlocked.

The text was from none other than Caesar. It read:

Lunch tomorrow at 2 p.m.?

Raelyn kicked off her heels and plopped down onto the king size bed. Instead of replying immediately she pondered on a response.

I don't know if us doing this is a good idea..., Raelyn sent off.

Two minutes later, Caesar responded with: *Most things we try are never as bad as we thought they'd be. Take a chance. I promise I won't waste ya time...*

Raelyn carefully thought about his offer. Kicking it with Caesar behind Jett's back was risky. However, she couldn't deny her attraction towards the handsome, mysterious stranger. *Jett will kill me if he finds out*, Raelyn told herself. *But you only live once*, her conscience whispered.

Raelyn read the last line in Caesar's final text again. *Would it be so bad if I tried something different*, she asked herself. Jett was all she'd ever known…but lately his routine was becoming tiring.

Take a chance, the tiny voice in her mind said.

Without further hesitation, Raelyn sent a simple one word response to him that sealed the deal. *Where?*

***

Blue and Zac pulled inside the parking garage of her apartment building. She'd spent the entire day with him and now it was finally time to get back to the real world. Regret was the furthest thing on her mind. On one hand, Blue wanted to be with Zac. Yet on the other, she was afraid of what starting over would be like. *I've given my heart to Deon for three whole years and look where we are now*, she thought.

Accepting that Blue still needed a little time to figure things out, Zac decided it was finally time to go back to Miami. Of course, he extended an invite to her if and when she was finally ready for something real.

"I hope I see you soon," Zac said, switching the gears to park. He turned and looked at Blue, silently wondering how she'd effortlessly managed to steal his heart. *I just hope I don' get played in the end trying to be patient*, Zac thought.

"I'm sure you will," Blue smiled. Her attention suddenly shifted to the steel bat coming directly at the back window.

KSSSSSSSSSHHHHHHH!

Glass shattered and sprayed the leather seats in the back after a steel bat came crashing through the window!

FIFTEEN

BOOM!

BOOM!

BOOM!

Deon's steel bat came down hard on Zac's beautiful Rolls Royce, denting in the metal with each brutal blow.

"*Ayyyyeeeee*! WHAT THE HELL ARE YOU DOING?!" Zac screamed, fumbling with his seatbelt.

"Oh my God! Deon, *NO*!" Blue yelled.

As soon as Zac jumped out the car, Deon took a swing at his skull. Thankfully, he dodged it, causing him to smash the driver's window.

"You thought shit was a game, nigga?!" Deon screamed, taking a second swing.

Zac quickly ducked that one as well. He figured Deon had a temper but he didn't expect him to go all Babe Ruth on his ass.

"You gon' come up here! Fuck my girl, sleep in my bed, and act like shit's all good! Nah, nigga! You got me fucked up!"

Blue quickly hopped out and rounded the car. "Deon, please stop!" she pleaded.

"Man, fuck you, Blue!" Deon sneered, pointing the bat at her. "My mama told me yo' ass would never amount to shit. But like a fuckin' idiot I stick around! I don't know how I ever tolerated yo' lyin' ass."

"*Tolerate*?" Blue repeated skeptically. "Mothafucka, you wanna talk about tolerating some shit? Tolerating is putting up with you and your bullshit for so long, Deon. Every time we fall out, you always runnin' back to your mama tellin' her I'm doin' this and that. Nigga, I take care of your broke ass," Blue reminded him. "If ya mama can do a better job at it, then take ya ass back there."

"Fuck you! I will!" Deon spat.

"Great. Make my life easier," Blue said.

Zac looked at the damage at his car then back at Deon.

"That bitch yo' headache now, bruh," he said, tossing the bat and walking off. "I'll be back in the mornin' to get my shit."

***

Symba strutted across the floor behind the bar as she collected bottles to mix and make drinks. She'd been bartending at The Pink Kitten Gentlemen's Club for two years, and it earned her a pretty decent minimum wage. The tips were great, and she'd met some of her best orgasms there.

Symba looked enticing in a black leather bustier and black high-waist skin tight shorts. Her long, shapely legs were covered in mesh stockings, adding to her appeal threefold. She was so sexy that she damn near put the dancers to the shame—which was part of the reason niggas couldn't stay out her face.

Just as Symba was pouring up a mixed drink for a customer, her cellphone buzzed on her hip. After seeing the caller was Canyon, Symba snuck off to the side and answered.

"What's up? I'm at work," she said.

"You can't be too busy. You answered," Canyon teased.

"Whatever," Symba giggled.

"Shit, I'm just fuckin' with you. Where you work wit' all dat music in the background though?"

"I bartend at The Pink Kitten in Buckhead," Symba told him.

"Oh,word? I'ma have to pull up on you tonight."

"I'll be here," Symba smiled. "But hey, I have to get back to work. I'll be on the lookout for you."

"Same."

Symba quickly disconnected the call before her manager saw her fucking off on the clock. The night went like any other, and shit didn't really start picking up until around 11 p.m.

From the bar, Symba watched as a few of the dancer flocked to a small group of men who'd just entered. *Must be some celebrities*, she thought.

Symba pushed her breasts up in her bustier, hoping to gain extra tips from the niggas with the real paper. Her gesture quickly caught the attention of a regular. Thirty-two old Ron never missed an opportunity to flirt with the chocolate Goddess. As a matter of fact, Symba was the only reason he frequented The Pink Kitten.

"You'd be a nigga's weakness," Ron said, pumping Symba up more than she already was.

She was just about to respond when she noticed Canyon in the background. Apparently, it was him and his crew that was causing all the commotion. *This man just gotta make an entrance*, she thought to herself smiling.

"What can I get you, Ron?" Symba asked, focusing her attention back on her customer.

"Let me get a double shot of Hen and a Budweiser," he said. "And ya number too so I can take you out to dinner sometime."

Symba gave her best fake smile. Not only was Ron's approach whack, he also wasn't her type physically. "How about this," she said. "I'ma get you your drink first then we'll discuss the rest."

After shooing off a few groupies, Canyon swaggered over to the bar after spotting Symba. She didn't notice him approaching since she was busy grabbing a bottle from the cooler. Canyon couldn't take his eyes off her round, pear shaped ass. *She ain't got no clue what she doing to a young nigga*, he thought.

Ron was still trying to get on by the time Canyon walked up and that instantly irritated him. Ever the Scorpio, he'd always been the jealous type.

"Uh, excuse me, bruh," Canyon said, bossing his way in front of him. "What's up, babe?"

As soon as Symba saw Canyon, Ron instantly became invisible. Canyon looked handsome and casual in a Versace embroidered Medusa t-shirt, cargo khakis, and black and gold Giuseppe sneakers. The gold Emporio Armani watch on his wrist glistened in the club. As usual, Canyon was fresher than a newborn baby.

"I didn't think you were gonna actually come," Symba smiled.

Finally getting the hint, Ron sauntered off in irritation.

"I guess ya boy was feelin' some type of way," Canyon chuckled.

Symba waved Ron off and laughed. "He'll be alright," she said.

Suddenly, a cute light-skinned stripper by the name of Pleasure walked up and handed Symba a crisp hundred dollar bill. "The boys by the stage need a bottle," she said in a thick Hispanic accent. She then looked up and winked at Canyon who smiled in return.

Unenthused, Symba took the cash from Pleasure who purposely brushed her fingers along Symba's hand. She'd been flirting with the bartender ever since she got hired two months ago. Althugh Symba was flattered her bisexual days had long ended after college. Women were just too much fucking drama. Raelyn and Blue were more than enough.

Canyon didn't miss the flirtatious gesture between the two women.

"No tip?" Symba asked her.

Pleasure shrugged her shoulders before switching off.

"I got'chu," Canyon said, reaching in his pocket. Before Symba could decline, he handed her a crisp Franklin.

Symba smiled, gratefully taking the large tip. "Thank you," she said, tucking it her bosom.

"Aye, let's get up outta here," Canyon said. "I know this ain't really how you tryin' to spend ya Sunday evening?"

"Not really, but I can't just walk out of here with you. I'm on the clock," Symba told him.

"Oh yeah? Where ya manager at?" Canyon suddenly asked. "Let me rap wit' 'em for a second."

With a confused expression, Symba pointed to the slender, bald brother conversing with a fellow business man towards the back of the club. In silence, she watched as Canyon swaggered over to the owner and politely introduced himself. Within seconds, they were laughing and politicking like they were good old friends.

Apparently, money really does talk, Symba thought.

A few minutes later, Canyon returned to the bar with a slight grin on his face. The manager had no problem with releasing Symba early after Canyon committed to buying out the entire bar. A favor for a favor was the best trade.

"I'm ready to roll out when you are," Canyon told Symba.

SIXTEEN

I know she's a freak...I know that she freakin'...

I know she's a freak...Super freak...

So please do not try to run game on me...

Please do not try to run game on me...

Then she told me...She don't wanna be a freak no more...

She don't wanna be a freak no more...

Migos "*Freak No More*" blared through the massive speakers inside of the U-Bar in Camp Creek. Holding firmly onto Symba's hand, Canyon navigated through the thick crowd of people towards the VIP. After taking her to change, they headed over to the popular bar for drinks and entertainment.

Meanwhile across the club, a cute brown-skinned chick with shoulder length hair looked in their direction. "Kaleesi, is that your baby daddy?" she asked, squinting extra hard.

Natara and Kaleesi were seated at the bar when the young thug walked in with his new companion. Snapping her neck in the direction Natara was looking, Kaleesi eagerly scanned the crowd.

"Hell yeah, that's him. But who the fuck he with?" she asked with distaste.

Standing at a mere 5"3, Kaleesi was a pretty girl with honey skin, wide eyes, and heart-shaped lips that she kept coated in MAC. Black, French, and Italian, she had a headful of soft, jet black hair that reached the middle of her back. Curly baby hairs aligned the edge of her forehead, making her look even more exotic.

Her perky size C breasts and plump ass was paid for compliments of her baby daddy. And truth be told, Canyon never appreciated her flaunting both all around town—whether they were together or not.

"Look like some new thot he entertainin'," Natara instigated. "That mediocre bitch ain't got shit on you though." For years, they thrived off pumping one another up. "You think he brought her 'cuz he knew you were gonna be here?"

Kaleesi shook her head. "No. We ain't spoke in a couple weeks," she admitted. "He had no idea I was gonna be here tonight. But he's definitely 'bout to now," she said, climbing out the barstool.

Natara smiled wickedly, anxious to see some drama unfold. "*Ooh-wee*. Don't hurt her girl," she laughed.

Kaleesi was on one as she pushed through the crowd of people to get to Canyon and Symba. Ratchet by nature, she had no issue turning up in public. Canyon knew it. Natara knew it. And now the bitch booed up with her baby daddy was about to know it.

Canyon and Symba were nestled in a VIP booth, sharing a bottle of champagne and hookah without a care in the world. But all that quickly came to an end when Kaleesi barged inside.

"Really, Canyon?" Kaleesi asked, looking from Symba to Canyon. "You just stroll up in here with some bitch like we ain't kickin' it? I can't believe you! You ain't never tell me you was seeing somebody new."

Symba looked over at Canyon in confusion. "Who is she?"

Kaleesi held up her left hand, showing off the magnificent $200,000 10.05-carat diamond ring. "I'm the bitch you sharing him with," she said, sarcasm dripping in her tone.

When Canyon didn't respond fast enough, Symba stood to her feet. "No need," she said before walking out the VIP.

Canyon made a move to go after her, but Kaleesi quickly stepped in front of him and started turning up. Looking over her small stature, he watched as Symba disappeared into the crowd.

Fuck me.

***

Symba wasted no time hailing a cab back home. On the ride there, she cursed herself for ever thinking Canyon could be different. *That's exactly why I use these niggas for what they're worth. A nut and a meal.*

I'm so good.

Symba was five minutes into the drive when Canyon called her cell. Not wanting to be bothered, she sent a simple text that read: *Lose my number*. Afterwards, she powered off her phone completely. "Tuh! Is he serious?"

"Excuse me?" the African cab driver said, looking in the rearview mirror. Honestly, he just wanted an excuse to steal a glance at Symba.

Shaking her head, she continued to stare out the back window. To say she was embarrassed when Kaleesi flashed her engagement ring was an understatement. *These niggas ain't shit*, Symba thought in disgust.

***

After telling Kaleesi about herself, Canyon settled back in the booth alone with his bottle and bitter thoughts. Although he smashed his baby mama from time to time, there were no real ties between them other than the ring she still loved to flaunt.

Years earlier, Caesar had warned him about wifing a hood hoe, but Canyon had to learn the hard way. Instead of cutting things loose when he had a chance, Canyon carelessly put a baby up in her. Major mistake…but he didn't regret the blessing that came from it.

Damn, I can't believe she ran Symba off like that though, Canyon thought. *I guess I should've warned her in advance I gotta few exes crazy enough to fight her.*

Since Canyon and Kaleesi shared a beautiful four year old daughter, he had no choice but to put up with his crazy baby mama for the sake of their seed. Kaleesi was hopeful they would one day have the storybook wedding she dreamt of.

Canyon, however, had another agenda. He'd proposed a few months after Kaela was born in hopes of solidifying them as a family. But Kaleesi's out of control behavior was one he couldn't settle with for the rest of his life. Canyon tried to break things off as peacefully as he could, but peace didn't exist when it came to Kaleesi.

In aggravation, Canyon watched as she danced on some nondescript nigga in an attempt to make him jealous. She was already undressed in a black cage dress. The sides were cut out so any guy could clearly see she was pantiless.

Canyon finally had enough of her antics after Kaleesi's admirer grabbed on the $10,000 ass he'd paid for. Jumping off the leather sofa, he stormed over to his baby's mother and snatched up her little ass up without hesitation.

"What is wrong with you?" Kaleesi asked, acting as if she didn't know what was up.

Once they were outside in the parking lot, Canyon turned her loose and gave it to her. "I'm tired of you tryin' to fuck up my name, Leesi. All that shit in there was uncalled for. Hell, I can't even go out and have a drink without bumpin' into you on some bullshit."

"Not with another bitch you can't," Kaleesi childishly retorted, tossing her hands on her hips. "I mean, what type of shit is that? You don't want me seeing no other niggas but you can parlay with these hoes?"

"I told you I didn't want no niggas around my daughter. I never said you couldn't date," Canyon told her.

"Whatever. I stand corrected by my motherfucking actions. And any bitch I see you with gon' get the same damn treatment."

To be so little, Kaleesi was feisty as hell—which was one of the qualities that initially attracted Canyon. Now it was just a burden.

"Man, get in the fuckin' car," Canyon demanded. "I'm takin' ya ass home. I'm done even talkin' 'bout this shit."

"But I rolled with my girl—"

"Now you rollin' out with me," Canyon said. "Now shut yo' ass up and get in the ride. I ain't finna ask you again."

Kaleesi's kitty jumped in her panties. She loved whenever her baby's daddy talked bossy. *That bitch would never know how to handle a nigga like Canyon*, she thought climbing into his Bugatti.

SEVENTEEN

BOOM!

BOOM!

BOOM!

Blue's eyes instantly shot open after the loud banging on her front door. Looking over to her left, she half-expected to see Deon—or even Zac. What she wasn't expecting was to wake up alone. "Damn," she muttered, running a hand through her hair.

BOOM!

BOOM!

BOOM!

Groaning in frustration, Blue climbed out the bed and padded barefoot to the front door. *I forgot this nigga said he was coming to get his shit in the morning.*

Without peeking through the peephole, Blue absentmindedly opened the front door.

Pamela Atkinson rudely barged inside with a huge tan Michael Kors tote by her side. Her long, dark brown hair was pulled back in a ponytail and as usual her face was beat for the Gawds.

At fifty-five years old, Deon's mother was absolutely beautiful. She worked as a deacon at a local mega church, but was as phony and judgmental as they came.

From the first day Deon brought Blue home, Pam didn't like her. Ghetto and classless was what she'd labeled the young girl, but still her son couldn't stay away.

"Well, good morning to you," Blue said, closing the door behind her.

"Now I ain't got all day. Where's Deon's stuff? He said it'd already be packed so I can grab and go," Pam rattled off. Looking around the house, she didn't once make eye contact with Blue. She loathed the sight of her son's girlfriend just that much.

"I thought Deon would have come to pack his own stuff," Blue said.

Pam finally looked up at Blue, disgusted by the sight of her in an oversized tee. She never appreciated the way her son painted her to be. "See, this the stuff I'm talking about," Pam said, shaking her head. "Had Deon never left home we wouldn't be going through all this in the first place. But, no. He wanna go off and do him. He's gon' learn though. I told his ass 'keep the strays in the streets'. 'Cuz this is what it gets you."

Oh hell no. I know this woman ain't trying to turn up on me, Blue thought. "Um…I'ma act like

I didn't hear that," she said. "Plus, Deon's a grown man. Or did you not notice?"

"And that's another problem you seem to have," Pam told her. "You disrespectful. But I get it. Deon told me all about ya crack head mama. And like they say, 'if it's somethin' wrong with the bitch, it's somethin' wrong with the pup'."

Blue's cheeks instantly turned beet red. Her mother was a sensitive subject, and she was two seconds from slapping the elder woman.

"It's all in the way you were raised," Pam continued.

"Look, I don't need to be further insulted by a woman who knows nothing about me," Blue snapped. "Just get Deon's things and go!"

Pam smiled maliciously before shaking her head and walking off.

Old bitch, Blue cursed. *Why couldn't Deon have come to get his own shit? Why did he have to send reinforcements?*

Blue was just about to take a seat on the jade sofa to calm down when nausea suddenly washed over her. Clasping a hand over her mouth, Blue rushed to the nearest bathroom, dropping to her knees in front of the toilet.

BWWUUURRRRGGHHHH!

Blue heaved the contents of her stomach until she was spitting up mere stomach acid. Hearing all the commotion, Pam went to the bathroom to see what was wrong.

Frowning in the doorway, she crossed her arms and looked down at Blue in disappointment. "Great. Don't tell me you pregnant now too."

***

"So I know I asked before but you kinda danced around the answer," Caesar told Raelyn the following afternoon. The two were seated at a table on the outdoor patio of *Six Feet Under*, enjoying lunch and the warm Georgia weather.

Raelyn knew what the question was going to be well before he even asked. Unfortunately, she didn't have enough time to prepare for it.

"What does buddy do for a livin'?"

Caesar's sudden curiosity in Jett made her uncomfortable. The last thing she wanted to do was talk about her man while on a date with another. "Really?" Raelyn asked, totally caught off guard by the unexpected question.

Since the robbery, he'd become a bit more interested in her significant other. The fact that Raelyn also couldn't give him a straight answer raised his suspicions even more. “I told you before. I’m just tryin’ to see what the competition lookin’ like,” he joked.

“There is no competition—on either end,” Raelyn quickly added. She looked up to see him smirking at her, apparently trying to read her thoughts. “You asked me to eat with you and I agreed. I’m sorry but a steaming plate of oysters and shrimps is not gonna make me call off my engagement. Neither is probing me for info so you can one-up Jett.”

Ouch. Just the sound of hearing the motherfucker’s name rubbed him the wrong way. However, Caesar tried his best to keep his composure. “That ain’t my intentions at all,” he said politely. “But since I can see it upsets you, I’ll drop it…for now,” he added.

Rae cut her eyes at Caesar. Immediately, she wondered why he was so curious about Jett.

***

“Aye, I could be trippin’, bruh. But ain’t that Raelyn over there?” Roman asked, looking out at the dining section. He, Jett, and Ace were at the bar on the rooftop entertaining some chicks they had met at the mall when he spotted his homeboy’s girlfriend.

Upon hearing Raelyn's name, Jett quickly turned his attention away from the dark-skinned cutie he was conversing with. His heart instantly plummeted to the pit of his stomach after seeing his beloved fiancee talking and laughing with some guy on the patio.

Jett immediately peeped his expensive jewelry and designer wear. "Who the fuck is this nigga?" he asked angrily, his fists clenching.

Ace's jaw muscle tensed as well. He wasn't feeling the sight of Raelyn all booed up with some new dude. Seeing her with Jett everyday was enough already.

"Um…excuse me?" Jett's date asked. "Aren't you supposed to be kickin' it with me? Why you staring at ole girl like she Sunday Night football or some shit?"

Jett didn't respond as he stared daggers at Caesar. He could smell the nigga's cologne from where he sat so he knew without a doubt that Raelyn had been seeing him for some time.

"I'm out," Jett's date said, standing to her feet.

Ace's companion slid out her seat as well and left with her girl. However, Roman's 20-year old date stayed right where she was planted.

"Come on, Ashley. What are you doing?"

Ashley waved her girls off. “Damn that. I’ma get my free meal,” she said. “I’ll get up with ya’ll later.”

Shrugging their shoulders, they walked off leaving the two men alone. Jett continued to stare Rae down from where he sat. I can’t believe this bitch would even step out on me, he thought to himself. Suddenly, the shoe didn’t feel so good on the other foot.

For years, he’d been cheating on Raelyn right under her nose without the slightest hint of regret. He figured what she didn’t know wouldn’t hurt her. Now Jett was finally getting a dose of his own medicine, and it left a bitter taste in his mouth.

Reaching over, Jett grabbed the knife on the table, tempted to pull a Jay-Z on that ass. However, Ace quickly stopped him. “Not here, dawg.”

Pissed beyond reasoning, Jett stood to his feet. He couldn’t take the sight of Caesar and Raelyn any longer so he decided to leave. “Follow da nigga,” he said through clenched teeth. “I wanna know exactly who da mufucka is.”

With that said, Jett stormed off, angrily shoving a guy who was accidentally standing in his way. Unfortunately, Raelyn had no idea the dilemma she had just caused.

EIGHTEEN

It was 2:17 p.m. when Symba heard knocking on her front door. She wasn't expecting company so she didn't know who could've been at that time of day. She'd talked to Blue on the phone earlier and Raelyn had been MIA since the *Compound.*

Symba had just taken out some vegetables to chop up for an omelet. Ever the night owl, she ate her breakfast when most people were probably done with their lunch. Her iPod was plugged into the speaker, and Jhene Aiko's soulful voice filled the room.

"I wonder who that could be," Symba said, heading towards the front door. As soon as she peered through the peephole and saw Canyon, her breath instantly caught in her chest. *He's a lot bolder than I thought he would be*, she thought.

Swallowing her reservations, Symba unlocked and opened the front door. "You got a lot of nerve coming here," she said. Her eyes then wandered to his Bugatti parked in front of her house. "Ya wife ain't out there waiting to pounce is she?"

Canyon slowly stepped inside Symba's home, keeping his intense gaze locked on her. Without a word, Canyon pulled off his $700 J. Crew jacket on tossed it on her sofa. Before she knew what was happening, he pulled her close and kissed her.

Symba wanted to pull away and make him work for it after the shit last night. However, she knew was going to give him some the minute she saw him standing outside. Whether he knew it or not, Canyon had her pussy in control.

Fuck him for being so damn irresistible.

Symba melted into Canyon's embrace as he held firmly onto her tiny waist. His touch, his taste, and his fragrance was intoxicating.

I hope she don't think that I think that she some kind of hoe…

'Cuz I don't care…That just let me know that she knows what she wants…

Jhene Aiko and Miguel's collabo track played on low as they two indulged in a passion-filled kiss. The door to Symba's house was wide open for the entire neighborhood to see their affection. But closing it was the last thing on her mind.

Symba didn't protest when Canyon lifted her up and carried her to the first bedroom in the home. It was the guest, but it didn't matter to either one of them.

Gently, Canyon laid her down on the mattress before pulling off his fitted white V-neck. Symba eyed his rock hard abdomen and buff chest.

She then softly ran her fingertips over the scar on his torso. Leaning forward, she placed a delicate kiss there before creating a trail that led down to the button of his jeans.

In anticipation, Canyon watched as Symba took her time unfastening his jeans. His dick was so hard that she could clearly see the imprint through his designer jeans. Sliding them down his athletic legs, Symba eased his boxers down immediately after.

Her mouth instantly watered at the sight of his curved, thick pole standing at attention. Taking it in her small hand, she stroked it gently before placing a wet kiss on the tip.

Determined to stay in control, Canyon softly pushed her back in the bed and lowered himself at her waist. Teasing her unmercifully, he ran his tongue over the thin fabric covering her pussy. That immediately drove Symba wild.

"Mmm. What are you doing to me?" she whispered, arching her back.

Taking his time, he slid her panties down before French kissing her button. Symba's toes curled as Canyon's long tongue worked magic on her clit.

"*Ooh*, shit!" Symba whimpered. When it began feeling too good, she tried to inch away but Canyon firmly held her in place. "Oh my God! I'ma cum!" Symba bellowed.

"Nah, not yet," Canyon said, climbing in between her legs.

"Shit, I wanna feel you so bad," Symba whispered.

Leaning down to kiss her, Canyon rubbed his thick mushroom shaped head over her wet pussy. Symba bucked her hips forward, loving the feel of it massaging her pearl.

"Stop playing with me Canyon," Symba begged. She couldn't take any more of the teasing. She had to feel him inside of her. She had to experience what an orgasm by him felt like. "I need you…"

Canyon didn't think it was possible for his dick to grow any harder until he heard those three words. "If I put this mufucka in, its mine. You hear me?"

Symba continued to grind on his hard pipe, desperate for him to enter her at all costs. "Yes daddy," she whispered.

Pleased with her response, Canyon slid a few inches inside her slick opening. Symba moaned and shivered upon his entrance. Even with all the screwing she did, her kitty miraculously managed to stay tighter than a virgin.

Staring deeply into Symba's eyes, Canyon slowly stroked her into ecstasy. "As long as you real with me, I'ma always be a hunnid with you," he told her.

Symba's pussy grew wetter with each stroke, and she could feel a premature orgasm approaching. "What about your wife?" she whispered

Without warning, Canyon pulled out and flipped Symba onto her stomach. "What wife?" he asked, plunging into her from behind.

Symba dropped her head in pure euphoria as she grabbed the bed sheets. Canyon felt so good inside; he made sinning a beautiful thing. *Damn him.*

"I don't wanna get hurt, Canyon," Symba moaned.

Canyon kissed and nibbled on her shoulder, causing chills to run down her spine. His large hands held her small waist as he dipped in and out. Symba was so wet that her juices covered his six-pack. *Pussy so good make a nigga wanna wife her*, he thought in satisfaction.

"You won't," Canyon promised her.

"Damn, I'm about to cum!" Symba exclaimed.

Speeding up his pace, Canyon ferociously pumped her from the back, determined to climax with her. "Gon' head. Cum," he coached, dipping a finger in her tight asshole.

That immediately drove Symba nuts. Unable to hold back, she finally released a strong orgasm that left Canyon's dick soaked.

Seconds later, he snatched out, releasing his warm load all over Symba's round ass. Winded, Canyon collapsed beside her and struggled to catch his breath. *Shit, I prolly shouldn't have gone in raw*, he thought afterwards. But it was too late now. Tripping up was how he'd gotten stuck with Kaleesi in the first place.

"What are your plans for the day?" Canyon asked breathlessly

Their sex permeated the air, reminding them of the epic fuck-fest that had recently come to a close.

Rolling over, Symba turned around to face him. She hesitated a little before she finally spoke. "Canyon, look…I gotta be real with you. I like you and all…but I don't think it's a good idea for you to get too comfortable with me."

"You for real?"

"Dead ass," Symba said. "Honestly, I'm just not trying to get caught up right now."

Canyon remained silent for several seconds as he thought about what she was saying. "Aight," he finally said. "I can respect that."

After establishing that, Symba decided to change the subject in order to ease the tension.

"So what is it you do?" she asked curiously. His occupation had been a curiosity of hers since the day they'd met.

Canyon's jaw muscle tightened after the question he knew would pop up sooner or later. "Distribution," he said simply.

A perfectly arched brow rose at his response. "Really?" Symba asked in skepticism. The nice clothes, expensive jewelry, and fancy car were finally beginning to make sense.

"Yeah, I'm the manager at a warehouse," Canyon told her.

Symba wasn't expecting him to add that, and her expression showed it. "Where?" she asked, with a look that said she didn't believe him for a second. Canyon pushed a million dollar car. Not even a managerial position could afford that.

"Coca Cola," Canyon quickly said. "But look, enough about me. I ain't makin' no noise, shawty. I'm tryin' to hear about you. What's up? Where you from? Where you grew up?"

"Decatur. You?"

"Brooklyn."

Symba looked surprised. "Really? How long you been down here?"

“Me and my patnah moved down here ‘bout ten years ago,” Canyon said, reminiscing on the past.

A sudden increase in demand had propelled the duo to up and relocate. Caesar’s cousin continued to hold shit down in NY, while they singlehandedly took over shit in the South. With quality product and better prices, the local competition had no choice but to jump on board or bow down.

As expected, they made a few enemies. The small dime-sized scar on Canyon’s rib was a painful reminder of the cost of power.

“Well…now you know more ‘bout me,” Canyon began. “Tell me somethin’ I don’t know yet ‘bout you.”

Symba hesitated as she bit her bottom lip. “Well…you remember that game we played back at your condo…?”

“Yeah.”

“During the time when you guessed if I was a daddy’s girl…I lied…”

Canyon slowly turned to face Symba. He wasn’t expecting to hear that.

“Before I lost my parents, I was really close to my dad,” she whispered. “He was the center of my life.”

"Damn ma. I'm sorry to hear that," Canyon told her. "I lost my pops at an early age too, so I know how that shit can be. We were real tight. Matter fact, he taught me everything I know."

There was a brief period of silence between them before Canyon spoke again.

"In a weird way, I'm low key happy you shared that with me," he told her. "Makes me feel like you lettin' me in."

"My trust isn't easily gained," Symba quickly said.

"Neither is mine," Canyon told her.

Symba opened her mouth to further inquire about his life, but was suddenly caught off when Canyon's cell began vibrating.

"Hold up. I gotta get this right quick," he told Symba. Climbing out the bed, he walked naked out the bedroom and answered. "Yo'."

"I think I may have some info on them cats," Lamont said, in regards to the robbery. " I ain't got much but it's a start."

"Fa'sho. Meet me at The Presidential in an hour," Canyon said before disconnecting the call. Walking back into the bedroom, he hastily proceeded to dress.

"You leaving?" Symba asked, trying her best not to sound disappointed.

"Yeah, I got some business to tend to," Canyon told her. "But I'ma get up with you later."

Canyon placed an affection peck on her forehead and promptly left the house.

Once she heard the front door close, Symba smiled to herself.

NINETEEN

Raelyn felt like she was on cloud nine as she strutted to her apartment unit. Although she knew seeing Caesar secretly wasn't in her best interest, she couldn't deny the chemistry that they had. So far he seemed like a cool, patient, levelheaded guy, but Rae knew there was more to him he wasn't letting on. She'd had yet to ask him what he did for a living.

Maybe he'll tell me when he feels the time is right.

"I really need to tread carefully though," Raelyn told herself. She knew if she wasn't careful she could possibly get caught slipping—but what she failed to realize was that it had already happened.

Sticking her key in the door, Raelyn pushed it open before stepping inside—

The unexpected brutal slap to her face sent her falling to the hardwood floors. Before Raelyn knew what was happening and why, Jett snatched her to her feet and dragged her towards the sliding glass doors.

"Jett, what are you doing?!" Raelyn cried. Her left cheek was red and puffy after the devastating hit. Mascara ran down her cheeks, and the vice grip Jett had on her hair was unbearable.

Ignoring Raelyn, he snatched the glass doors open leading to the outdoor patio. Her eyes instantly shot open in fear; she had no idea what Jett planned on doing next.

"JETT, PLEASE STOP!" Raelyn screamed, her voice cracked with emotion. "You're scaring me!"

High out of his mind on coke and LSD, Jett dragged his girlfriend towards the patio railing kicking and screaming.

"JETT! STOP!"

Snatching her hair, he slammed her against the glass rail and held over by her collar. "I saw you today with that mufucka!" he screamed, his eyes red-rimmed and tear-filled. Raelyn knew his ass was crazy so he didn't know why she was foolish enough to actually try him.

Glancing over her shoulder, Raelyn looked down at the traffic below. "Jett, please!" she cried, unable to bear the thought of falling. "I'm so sorry! Please, stop!" Tears slipped from her eyes and plummeted thousands of feet.

"Yeah, I'm sorry too," Jett said grief-stricken. "Sorry I ever trusted yo' ass!"

"Jett, please! I swear I'll never do it again!" Raelyn cried. "Just please let me go! You're scaring me!"

"Fuck was you thinkin', huh? What? I ain't good enough?" Jett spat. "You lookin' for a mufucka to come save you?"

"No," Raelyn sobbed.

"Where the nigga at now?" Jett asked.

"Jett, I'm sorry! Please don't let me fall!"

Suddenly, Ace and Roman rushed inside the condo, stopping Jett before he could push Rae over.

"Man, what the fuck is wrong with you?" Ace asked, shoving Jett.

Raelyn slid to the ground and tried her best to regain her breathing. She'd never been so afraid in her life. At that moment, she knew she needed to get far away from Jett for the sake of her safety.

"What's wrong with me? Fuck nigga, what's wrong wit'chu?" Jett retaliated, pushing him back. "I done told yo' mufuckin' ass 'bout steppin' in my shit—"

"Bruh, you high as fuck! Wildin'!" Ace told him. "All these got damn white folks that live here, cuz, is you crazy?!"

While Ace and Jett argued on the patio, Raelyn took that as her cue to bounce. She didn't grab anything on the way out, only her purse that been strewn across the floor.

Realizing that his girl was leaving, Jett pushed Ace out the way and ran after her. Raelyn was already halfway down the hall when he stepped out. "If you leave me for dat nigga, you 'bout as dead to me as him, Rae!" Jett yelled.

"I'm good with that!" Raelyn tossed over her shoulder. She was still shaken up by the patio nightmare. And all she wanted was to get as far away from Jett as possible.

"Fuck you then, bitch!" Jett spat. He was acting ratchet as hell in the hallways of his luxury condo but he didn't care. He wanted Raelyn to be as hurt as he was. Pulling out the ultimate weapon, Jett yelled, "That's why I been smashin' ya home girl, Symba."

Raelyn automatically froze in place. Initially, she figured he was only saying it to get under her skin, but then she thought about her friend's demeanor. There was nothing she could put past her.

"What the fuck did you just say?" Raelyn asked angrily, turning on her heel.

Now that the damage was done, Jett walked back inside the condo slamming the door behind him.

Tears stung the back of Raelyn's eyes as she tried to digest what Jett had just told her. *Hell no. He gotta be lying*, Rae told herself. *My girl wouldn't do me like that*? *Would she*?

In tears, Raelyn ran to her Honda Coupe and climbed inside. After fastening her seatbelt, she pulled out her cellphone and called up Symba. She had to hear it from the horse's mouth.

On the fourth ring she finally answered. "What's up, girl? I'm getting ready for work. Can I hit you back later—"

"Is it true?!" Raelyn yelled in a quivering tone. "Have you been fucking Jett behind my back all this time?" Tears dripped off her chin and landed in her lap as she waited on a response. The silence was deafening.

Symba released a deep breath. "Raelyn…we need to talk…"

The fact that her best friend didn't deny it was all she needed to know it was true. "You know what, Symba. Ya'll motherfuckers belong together. Rot in hell, bitch. I'm through with you."

CLICK.

Overwhelmed with emotion, Raelyn started the ignition and pulled out the parking garage. Ironically, Jhene Aiko's "*The Worst*" was playing on the radio.

Meanwhile inside, Jett went on a total rampage, flipping over and trashing anything he could get his hands on. After destroying the 62" living room TV, Jett ran inside his master bedroom where he snatched all of Raelyn's clothes and shoes from the closet.

"This bitch got me all fucked up!" Jett yelled at no one in particular.

In silence, Ace and Roman stood back and allowed their boy to vent. He deserved that much. They did, however, intervene when he started chucking shit off the patio. Thousand dollar clothes and shoes plummeted thousands of feet below as he tossed Raelyn's items over the edge.

"Bruh, chill!" Ace said, pulling him back inside.

Jett was so distraught, he barely could contain himself. Losing Raelyn hurt worse than losing his own mother. And the fact that she was caught creeping with another nigga hurt twice as bad. All while he was running the streets entertaining random hoes, Rae was doing her own dirt. Just much more cleaner.

Pinching the bridge of his nose, Jett paced back and forth. He wanted to punch a wall; do anything to make him feel better. Thankfully, the next thing Roman said did.

"We found out a lil' somethin on dude too," he told him. "My nigga, you ain't gon' believe this shit."

TWENTY

Two Weeks Later.

Blue and Symba were seated at an outdoor table in Atlantic Station as they ate ice cream and caught up on the latest drama of their lives.

"So I just found out I'm pregnant," Blue said, taking a scoop from her double fudge sundae. She looked cute that afternoon in a scarlet crop top and midi skirt combo.

Symba snatched her sunglasses off and looked at Blue in surprise. "Get the fuck out!"

A few passerby's looked at Symba and scowled.

"Deon or Zac's…?"

Blue was just about to respond when she noticed a familiar face walking up the block. "Uh-oh. Don't look now."

Doing the exact opposite, Symba turned in her seat and frowned at the sight of Canyon with some new chick. The cute Asian he had his arm casually wrapped around was built like a sister. But honestly, Symba would've felt better seeing him with his baby mama.

The time that they spent together had become sparse, but she chucked it up as him being with work. Symba didn't want to believe Canyon had backed off after smashing. *He didn't seem like the hit it and quit type. But I don't be knowing what run through these motherfuckers' heads*, she thought.

"Well…?" Blue asked, snapping her back to reality.

"Well what?" Symba asked, confused.

"Well, ain't ya'll kicking it? You ain't gon' say shit?" Blue instigated. Had Raelyn been there, she would've been the balance to diffuse the situation. But sadly, she'd cut Symba off after discovering her disloyalty.

"We ain't serious like that," Symba said, waving it off. However, inside she felt a combination of anger and sadness. He talked a good game, but she could clearly see he was just like every other nigga; a dog. "It's all good—"

"*All good*? Bitch, I can look at your face and tell you hurt—"

"Blue, let it go," Symba finally said.

Tossing her hands up in mock surrender, she continued eating her fudge ice cream.

Symba took one final look at Canyon and his exotic companion, and shook her head.

"Couldn't be me," Blue said, looking down at her sundae.

Feeling as though she had something to prove to her friend and herself, Symba stood to her feet and walked over towards Canyon. He and his love interest were just about to walk in *H&M* when Symba stopped him.

"Um…Canyon?"

Symba instantly felt foolish and embarrassed the second he and his chick turned towards her. Canyon almost looked at her like he didn't know her. She was almost tempted to walk off with her tail tucked between her legs, but Symba was much stronger than that.

"Gon' head. I'll meet you inside," Canyon told his counterpart.

Stuffing his hands in his pockets, he walked over to Symba. "Wassup?" he greeted nonchalantly.

"*What's up*? I don't even hear from you no more," Symba said. "And now I run into you out here with some…" she allowed her voice to trail off before she said some shit she couldn't take back. "Canyon, you should've told me what you were on from the jump from that way I wouldn't have…"

"Wouldn't have what?" he pressed. "Shit, Symba, I really don't even know why you sweatin' me right now. Last I remember, you told a nigga not to get too comfortable with you. So why you trippin' when I take yo' advice?"

Symba looked at Canyon like she didn't even recognize him. She was upset with herself for falling for him in spite of what she told herself. Symba had revealed a side of herself to Canyon that people rarely if ever saw. "You know what?" she said, backpedaling away. "You right. Do you, Canyon."

Chuckling, he headed towards the department store. "That's all a nigga know how to do, ma."

Symba quickly blinked her tears away as she headed back over to Blue. Plopping down in her seat, the first thing she said, "Have you heard from Raelyn?"

Truth be told, Symba didn't want Blue to have the opportunity to ask what happened. She was too embarrassed to admit Canyon had shitted on her—like he'd probably done so many women before her. *Niggas really ain't shit.*

"No, she's been MIA for the last couple weeks," Blue told her. "Not answering any of my calls or texts. That shit with you and Jett must've really fucked her up," she said. "You know that shit wasn't right, Symba. As a matter of fact, it's pretty fucked up if you ask me—"

"Well, I didn't ask you," Symba told her. "Let's just drop the subject."

Blue looked over at her girl and shook her head. Karma was a motherfucker and Symba was definitely getting her dose of it.

I wonder what the hell Rae's ass is up to, Blue thought.

***

Astonished, Raelyn stared out her hotel window which overlooked the beautiful city of Dubai. If it were not for the extended jet flight, she would have thought it was all a dream. After all, it wasn't every day a handsome man took her out the country.

Caesar was the first guy Rae had ever shown interest in outside of Jett, and truthfully that scared and excited her at the same time. For the longest, Marlon was all she'd ever known and loved…but out of nowhere, Caesar slid into her life changing everything up completely.

He was sweet, kind, funny, and thoughtful. And although they'd spent a lot of quality time together, they had yet to sleep together. Thankfully, Caesar hadn't made any tactless attempts at trying to get the pussy.

Raelyn was grateful too because she didn't know if she was ready to take things to that level—

especially since Jett was the only person she'd ever slept with.

Caesar treated Raelyn with the utmost respect and even put her up in a 5 star hotel when she and Jett fell out. When she finally felt comfortable enough to, Caesar allowed her to stay in one of the guest rooms in his crib.

Raelyn never talked about the shit that went down with her and her dude, and Caesar didn't bother pressing. He was only glad that buddy had finally fucked up, allowing him the interception. Unlike, Jett, Caesar treated Raelyn like a queen.

Every morning she awoke to a hearty breakfast compliments of his hired chef. And every evening they dined out at 3+ star restaurants.

Raelyn enjoyed Caesar's company so much that she rarely thought about everything that had recently taken place. She also failed to find out what he did for a living. Although Rae knew she should've asked long ago, she was somewhat afraid to know the truth. Caesar was such a good guy and she didn't want anything to taint his image—including how he earned his income.

With wide eyes, Raelyn admired the breathtaking scenery while taking mental pictures in her head to remember forever. From where she stood, she could clearly see *The Burj Khalifa*—the planet's tallest structure.

No more than twenty minutes ago, Raelyn and Caesar arrived at the *Burj Al Arab*—the world's only seven-star hotel—in a pearl white Maybach Landaulet. Rae felt like a celebrity as she climbed out and entered the building.

Jett had spoiled her…but Caesar pampered her so much that she almost felt guilty for accepting it…*Almost*.

Fixing the cuff links to his crisp white dress shirt, Caesar admired Raelyn's profile from behind. He'd even put most of his business back home on hold so he could spend time with Raelyn—and Canyon wasn't feeling that, especially when he was so close to figuring out who the guys were who robbed them.

Caesar didn't mind though. His boy could pout and business could wait. Whenever a woman had his attention, she really had *all* of it. And it was definitely rare for him to find a chick so bad she took up his whole week.

"You gon' admire the city from ya window the whole time we here?" Caesar asked humorously. "Why don't you go out and explore. Treat yaself to some shoppin'."

Raelyn turned around in time to see Caesar place his Visa on the plush King size bed. High-end satin sheets adorned the elegant piece of furniture. Caesar looked so handsome and fresh in dark fitted jeans, a dress shirt, and charcoal vest. The polished black Louboutin loafers on his feet were scuff-less and his Rolex glistened as usual.

"Why me?" Rae suddenly asked with a slight smile. She'd been wondering the question for some time now but had finally worked up the courage to ask. "I mean why are you treating me so special? And how long will this last so I don't get my hopes too high?"

Caesar scoffed before slowly approaching Raelyn. She had her hair pulled into a high bun atop her head, and he loved being able to see her beautiful face without restrictions.

Cupping Rae's chin in his hand, Caesar gently tilted her up to look in his eyes. "This the first and last time I'ma say this…" Without warning, he placed a gentle kiss on her plump lips. "I ain't that nigga, ma. And my time is too valuable to waste."

Raelyn's body melted into Caesar's as he held her closely. She'd told herself over and over again that she wasn't ready to get intimate with another man but he was making it incredibly hard.

"Why me?" she whispered, barely audible.

Caesar softly pinned his body against hers and interlocked their fingers. Raelyn could easily feel his thick rod through his dress pants, and it instantly made her clit throb. *He knows exactly what he's doing to me*, she convinced herself.

"'Cuz everything stopped the first time we made eye contact," Caesar admitted. "You seem poised, smart…but low-key contained. I can tell you ain't used to seein' the world."

Raelyn looked away in embarrassment, her cheeks turning beet red.

Touched by her sensitivity, Caesar gently tilted her chin upward and kissed her. "But that shit's all gonna change."

Raelyn hesitated before she spoke again. "This feels so right," she whispered. "But I don't wanna ruin anything by rushing, okay?"

Caesar smiled in amusement before placing an innocent peck on her forehead. She was so modest that he found it somewhat adorable.

"I'll meet you back here in a few hours so we can have dinner," he said, heading to the front door. "Don't get into too much trouble without me, aight?"

Raelyn gave a half smile before plopping down onto the bed. Her eyes slowly rested on the credit card after she heard the hotel door close. As soon as she reached for it, her cellphone rang.

Grabbing it off the nightstand, Rae looked to see who it was. "Hey, Blue," she answered unenthused. The two hadn't spoken in weeks and Rae was unsure if Symba had told her what happened. Sometimes she even wondered if Blue knew all along about Jett and Symba. She couldn't put shit past the bitches she *thought* were her best friends.

"*Hey, Blue*?" she repeated sarcastically. "Bitch, where the fuck you been? And what's been going on with you Symba?" she asked. "In my opinion, I really think you two should sit down and talk—"

"Blue, no offense. But I really ain't trying to hear no drama right now. I left that shit in the US, and I'm just trying to enjoy my little vacation."

"Ugh, bitch. Attitude. Where you at?" Blue asked, ever the nosey one.

"Dubai."

"Duh—what?"

Raelyn burst out laughing. "*Dubai*. Soaking up the sun and enjoying the company of a new male friend."

"*What*?! Excuse me? I'm must've had shit in my ears. Who the hell is this and what have you done with my girl? Parlaying in third world countries with strangers? The Rae I know would've never stepped out on Jett—much less with a nigga you just met."

"Yeah, and the Jett I *thought* I knew would've never stepped out on me," Raelyn retorted. She had a half of mind to tell Blue to mind her own business, but decided against it. "Look, I gotta go. I'll hit you up when I get back."

Before Blue even had a chance to tell her she was pregnant, Rae disconnected the call. The last person she wanted to hear about was Symba.

Slipping out of her clothes, Raelyn padded to the luxurious bathroom. After showering she planned on doing a little shopping and sight-seeing. All the drama back in Atlanta was the least of her worries.

TWENTY-ONE

Canyon brought his Bugatti Veyron to a slow stop in front of Symba's small Craftsman home. He hadn't heard from her since they last bumped into each other in Atlantic Station.

Shit, her car's here so she's gotta be home.

Canyon hadn't put much thought into the possibility of Symba having male company. He didn't feel like having to hem a nigga up, but he knew they needed to talk. Canyon knew he was a jack ass for the way he'd treated Symba, but just like she was trying to protect herself, he was doing the same.

Canyon figured it was finally time to lay the cards on the table. All the bitches he entertained were worth sacrificing if she were willing to take a chance on him.

Swallowing his reservations, Canyon skipped up the stone steps and rang Symba's door. He waited two whole minutes for a response before finally turning to leave. Yet just as he did the door cracked open.

"Aye, wassup? I hope I ain't catchin' you at a bad time. I was just in da 'hood…" Canyon lied.

"This is becoming a routine for you, huh?" Symba asked through narrowed eyes. "You fuck up then you pop up."

"Look, it ain't nothin' like that," Canyon told her. "But if you want me to leave—"

Without warning, Symba burst into hysterical cries.

Unsure of what he did to cause her reaction, Canyon rushed to Symba's aid. "Aye, what's up babe?" he asked, concern heavy in his tone.

Symba didn't protest when Canyon let himself in and held her close. So many emotions were running through her mind she could barely think. *I can't believe I let some dick tear me and my best friend apart*, she thought.

"Symba, talk to me."

Wiping her eyes, she sniffled. "Trust me. You don't wanna know."

Canyon's jaw tightened as he looked deep in Symba's eyes. They were a lot alike in more ways than one. "Try me," he said.

Symba paused as she debated on whether or not to open up. For fear of what he'd think she ultimately decided not to. "Oh my God. Look at me," she said, wiping her nose. "I'm so damn embarrassed. Standing here crying like a fucking baby."

Canyon gently brushed Symba's hair out of her face. She was so damn beautiful during her moment of vulnerability. All he wanted to do was hold her, and keep her safe. "Don't be," he said. "You good."

Symba sniffled and slowly walked over to her cream sofa. No man had ever seen her shed a tear, and there stood Canyon seeing her at her worst. "No, it's not," Symba said. "No, it's not okay. Nothing about me is fucking okay, Canyon. I'm a mess."

Joining Symba on the sofa, Canyon gently brushed his thumb across her cheek. He didn't know much about her, yet something kept him drawn to her. "Then let me clean you up…"

Symba silently watched Canyon stand to his feet and head towards her bathroom. Several seconds later, she heard the bath water run.

"What is he up to?" she asked herself. Symba was just about to climb off the couch when Canyon returned and lifted her into his strong tattooed arms.

Giggling the whole way, Symba allowed him to carry her inside the spacious bathroom. The room was warm and dim with only a single pod light on over the deep garden tub.

Where did he come from, Symba asked herself. *And most importantly how is he still here?*

Canyon took his time removing Symba's wardrobe. He could tell from her condition that she'd probably been wearing them for days, but he wouldn't dare speak on it. Once Symba was naked in all her magnificent glory, Canyon lifted her up and carried her to the spacious jet tub. As soon as he reached it, he carefully placed Symba inside the warm water. He didn't even mind getting his Givenchy tee a little wet.

After placing her inside, Canyon retrieved his cell and fished for a nice, mellow song to play. Seconds later, "ScHoolboy Q and Jhene Aiko's "*Fantasy*" filled the quiet room. Once the mood was set, Canyon removed his t-shirt and took a seat near the edge of the tub.

Symba marveled at his sculpted torso, eight pack abs, and scar on his rib. She knew there was a story to Canyon, and she could only hope he stuck around long enough for her to know it.

Keeping his gaze locked on Symba's, Canyon lathered her bath sponge with pomegranate body wash. Drawing her knees close to her chest, she could feel her body temperature slowly rising.

Canyon delicately ran the sponge down Symba's spine. In response, she shivered slightly. "What the hell are you doing to me, Canyon…?"

"Just tryin' to be here for you. I care about you, Symba."

She scoffed. "You barely know me.And if you did, I doubt you'd be this empathetic."

"Why do you do this?" Canyon suddenly asked.

"What?"

"Put up this barrier and shit," he said. "You right, I don't know much about you…and that's cool 'cuz I prefer learning more about you with time."

"Why?" Symba asked curiously. Canyon could have any bitch he wanted. Why was he was sticking around with her?

Canyon paused as he deliberated his response. "Because I feel like I met my match with you…," he admitted. "I feel like I finally met the female me, and it's a challenge—You a challenge. But I'm cool with that 'cuz you worth it."

Symba smiled bashfully and shook her head. "I won't compete for your love, Canyon," she told him. "I'm not that chick—"

"I'm not asking you to be," he said. "Matter fact, every bitch in my phone is history long as I'm the only nigga you feelin'."

Symba smiled. "Them hoes should've been history in that case…"

Canyon chuckled before leaning in to kiss her. Her body melted into his as she finally let her guard down for the first time ever. Receptive to her submission, Canyon lifted Symba from the water and carried her inside the master bedroom.

TWENTY-TWO

Raelyn tried her best to contain her excitement as she took a seat in the 4 star underwater hotel. Caesar had made reservations prior to the trip, so the two dined exclusively. Right beside their table was a huge plethora of sea life that she'd only seen on the Discovery Channel.

Raelyn had quite the adventure that afternoon so it felt good to relax and finally enjoy a meal. After Caesar left her alone to explore, she caught the taxi to the Dubai Mall to do some souvenir shopping and sightseeing. Two hours passed before Raelyn's feet finally got sore, so she headed back to the room—where she found a card on the bed next to a *Sak's Fifth* shopping bag.

Rae opened the letter and read the brief note from Caesar. The message was simple and to the point: *Meet me downstairs in the lobby at 6 p.m.*

Next Raelyn opened the shopping bag and pulled out a black and nude lace dress. The price tag on it was more than a monthly mortgage, and for a moment she hesitated accepting the pricey gift.

You only live once…

Instead of turning Caesar's generosity away, she slid out of her clothes and eased into the form-fitting dress.

One hour later, she was seated inside of *Al Mahara* with a man who was slowly but surely changing her life one day at a time.

After Caesar and Raelyn's first round of drinks arrived, she decided to initiate convo. "So…what are we really doing out here besides enjoying the beautiful scenery?"

It was Raelyn's first time asking the question. All afternoon she'd replayed Blue's words over and over again in her mind. As much as she didn't want to hear it, it was true. Raelyn didn't know the first thing about Caesar other than the fact that he was a good guy with a little paper—or at least portraying himself to be.

Get a grip Rae. No man takes a woman oversees just to flex. He may be the real deal, her conscious told her. Still, there was a side of Raelyn that was also cautious of his motives. *They say if something's too good to be true, it probably is.*

"I told you…business," Caesar simply said.

Raelyn wasn't expecting such a short response. "Um…okay. Let's try it this way…," she began. "What do you do for a living?"

"Are you sure you wanna know the answer to that?" he asked with a humorless expression.

"I wouldn't have asked if I didn't…"

Without a word, Caesar reached over and placed his hands over Raelyn's. Her hands were so small and soft in his, and he loved the way their complexions complimented one another.

"I like you, Rae. But my pops taught me at an early age to never reveal all your cards before knowing the other person's move."

"I wouldn't have stuck around this long just to bullshit you," Raelyn told him. "So why bullshit with me?"

Impressed with her response, Caesar sat back in silence a few seconds. Raelyn was a lot more mature than he expected her to be for her age. "Aight then," he said. "I own one half of an international drug trade business."

Raelyn started to laugh after assuming he was joking. However, the humorless expression on his face told her otherwise. Slowly, she retracted her hands. She couldn't say she was all too surprised. Yet it would've been nice to know sooner.

"Is there anything else I should know?" Raelyn asked, surprisingly poised.

"With you knowin' that, you now know everything," Caesar told her. "It's on you if you decide you wanna stick around."

Raelyn took a sip of her wine. "Well, I haven't gotten up and left yet. Have I?"

***

After a tasty dining experience at *Al Mahara's*, Caesar and Raelyn enjoyed the sunset while riding camels throughout the expansive desert. It was nearly 10 p.m. when they finally arrived at their final destination for the evening.

Zuma's had been the talk of the city for years; so Caesar couldn't pass up the opportunity to treat Raelyn to its signature Rubabu cocktails. After enjoying a few drinks and some conversation with an ex-pat couple they'd met, Caesar and Raelyn headed back to the *Burj Al Arab* for a night cap.

As soon as they reached their room, Raelyn noticed a bottle of sparkling wine on a silver tray in the middle of their bed. She was still somewhat tipsy from the cocktails from earlier, but luckily she knew how to hold her liquor while still conducting herself like a lady.

"I'm gonna go freshen up," Raelyn said, pulling off her heels. Her bare feet in the expensive, plush carpet felt like heaven. As a matter of fact, Rae felt like she was walking on clouds.

Their suite was set up similar to the bedroom of a king's palace, and Raelyn had never felt more royal in her entire life.

"Cool," Caesar replied, unbuttoning his shirt.

Raelyn quickly made her way inside the spacious bathroom. A huge bathtub was positioned in the center of the room surrounded by four marble pillars. On either side was a fancy, handcrafted bench with luxurious cloth seating.

Sighing deeply, Raelyn ran a hand through her wand-curled hair. She'd been kicking it with Caesar for a week straight, and all of the time spent together had finally led up to that point.

Calm down girl, Raelyn told herself over and over again. It's not like we haven't spent the night together. Yet it wasn't one bedroom…or one bed.

After freshening up, Raelyn slipped in a sexy dark blue pleated baby doll and pinned her hair up. Loose curls hung freely, framing her face perfectly. Upon giving herself a final once over, Rae slowly exited the master bathroom.

Caesar had some music playing on the iPod, and he looked a lot more comfortable in nothing but a crisp white wife beater and slacks. Sitting on the edge of the luxurious canopy style bed, he poured them both small glasses of wine. From where she stood, Raelyn admired Caesar's cocky chocolate arms and the tattoos that adorned his skin.

All you've been thinking about...

Do anything you want and let emotion rule your mind...

And now you say you dream about doing it anyway...

Oh yeah, just tell me what's on your mind...

Jeremih crooned as “Hold You Down” played on low, creating a calm and sensual atmosphere. Caesar knew just what he was doing.

“Come here,” he said in a low tone after noticing Raelyn staring at him.

Raelyn took her time walking over towards him. Her heart was beating so fast that she feared Caesar might hear it as well.

Handing her a glass of wine, he tried his best not to eye fuck her in her sexy little slip she wore. “Damn.” The word escaped his lips before he could even stop it.

“What is it?” Raelyn asked, taking a small sip of her wine.

“If you don’t know, ain’t meant for you to…”

Raelyn giggled before slowly stepping in between his legs. “What if I wanna know…?”

Caesar looked up at her with a serious expression on his handsome face. His hands gently slid up the length of her curved back. She was toying with him and she knew it. In one fluid motion, Caesar pulled her down on top of him. Surprisingly, Raelyn still managed to keep her grip on the wine glass, but some of its contents did splash onto the expensive bed sheets.

Moonlight poured into the suite as the two stared deeply into each other’s eyes. Without warning, Caesar leaned in and kissed her softly; his large hands slid down the length of her curvy body before settling on her round, plump ass.

While exploring Caesar's mouth with her tongue, Raelyn softly grinded her pelvis against his stiff erection. He was so hard that it made her pussy throb in anticipation, longing to be entered and dominated.

"I want you," Raelyn found herself whispering.

"You sure 'bout that?" Caesar asked, grabbing a handful of her pillow soft ass, his pole pressing into her flat belly.

Ignoring his question, Raelyn placed her wineglass on the night stand and straddled Caesar. Without a word, she pulled off her baby doll, revealing her full, perky breasts. Tan nipples stood at attention, making Caesar's mouth instantly water.

Sitting up, he placed delicate kisses along her collarbone and neck. "I promise I'll kill a mufucka before I let him hurt you." He touched the spot on her cheek where a bruise had recently healed. Caesar still had no idea that Raelyn's former boyfriend was behind the robbery.
"To tell you the truth, I'm glad dude fucked up," he said in between kisses. "You deserve a real nigga, Raelyn…"

Ignited from his words, she dropped down onto the mattress and slowly slid off her panties.

Raelyn was already wet when she slid her thighs apart for him to see her shaved kitty.

Caesar's dick strained against his dress pants as it begged for him to enter. Taking his time, he removed his clothes before dipping his head between her legs. First he wanted to be sure she tasted as good as she looked.

"*Caesar*," Raelyn gasped, after his tongue circled around her clit.

Pulling the hood back, Caesar teased her tiny button with the flick of his tongue. That immediately drove her crazy, seeing as she bucked against his face. After showing some much needed attention to her button, he curved his tongue up inside her as far as the length would allow. Catching her off surprise, he rolled it across her tight asshole a few times too.

"*Oooh*, that feels so good," Raelyn whispered, her cheeks bright red. Jett had never crossed that threshold before. But she had a feeling Caesar was about to put her on to a lot of new things she never discovered she liked.

Wiping his wet mouth with the back of his hand, Caesar climbed in between Raelyn's thighs. Resting his dick at the base of her mound, he stared deeply into her mint-colored eyes. "I ain't gon' never do you like that nigga," he promised.

"I know…," Raelyn smiled.

Caesar leaned down and kissed her passionately as he attempted to cross her threshold. Rae winced at his massive girth. She wasn't used to handling so much dick. Raelyn bit down on her bottom as she fought to accept the combination of pain and pleasure. Soon after, it quickly turned into pure euphoria.

"You fuckin' wit' a man now," Caesar whispered in her ear.

TWENTY-THREE

I hate rich niggas goddammit...

Cause I ain't never had a lot dammit...

Who you had to kill, who you had to rob?

Who you had to fuck just to make it to the top dammit?

J. Cole's "*Rich Niggaz*" poured through the speakers as Jett slowly eased his car inside the parking garage attached to his condominium. It was the first time he'd returned to the condo since he and Raelyn's fall out. Not wanting to face sleeping alone, Jett shared a bed with whatever female picked up the phone when he called. But now it'd been two weeks. And he needed to wash his ass, change his clothes, and get back to the money.

After parking, he climbed out and made his way to his unit. Jett sighed in disappointment the moment he opened the door. The place smelled of apple cinnamon.

"Raelyn..."

Jett couldn't deny that he felt like a total dumb ass for telling her he fucked Symba. He knew this time was different; he'd overstepped his boundary by playing with fire and now he was paying for it.

Pulling out his cellphone, Jett dialed Raelyn for the fiftieth time. As usual, he was sent straight to voicemail. Angered and bitter by the way shit had turned out Jett launched his phone at the wall.

"Fuck it. That bitch can go down with the mufucka too."

TWENTY-FOUR

Three Months Later.

Blue rubbed her swollen belly as she stirred a pot of steaming vegetables on the stove. Zac sat at the kitchen island behind her thumbing through a Forbes Magazine. After finding out about her pregnancy, he anxiously relocated to Atlanta to be there for Blue. Unbeknownst to her, he had plans on popping the big question after the baby was born.

Damn what Zachariah Sr. thought about Blue. She was the love of his life, and the woman he wanted to be with. "That smells great," he told her.

Blowing him a kiss over her shoulder, she continued with her wifely duties. It felt good to finally be appreciated by a man who knew her worth.

The two were so in tuned with one another that they didn't even hear the front door unlock and open.

"Bay, can you go in the closet and get me a roll of paper towels?" Blue asked. Truth be told, she was making a mess but Zac was grateful for the effort either way.

"Sure thing."

As soon as Zac stood to his feet, he instantly froze in place at the sight of Deon holding a loaded 9 mm. After hearing the chamber to the gun slide, Blue turned around as well—

"Deon?" she gasped, dropping the spatula to the tiled floor.

"You act like you surprised to see me," he said with a sinister grin.

Deon looked incredibly bad, and for a second Blue hardly recognized him. Heavy bags rested underneath his usually vibrant eyes and he looked like he'd even lost a little weight. Blue wasn't sure, but he looked like he was also using. From where she stood, she could clearly smell the heavy stench of liquor seeping from his pores. Apparently, their break up had taken a toll on him.

"Aye, man, take it easy," Zac said in a calm tone, trying his best to deescalate the situation. "Nobody has to get hurt."

Deon quickly aimed his heat at Zac. He'd been itching to end the motherfucker's life since they met.

"Deon, no!" Blue pleaded with tear-filled eyes.

He then aimed his weapon at the woman who was once the love of his life. "I can't believe you went and got pregnant by this fuck nigga,

Blue," Deon said. "It was supposed to be us until the end of time."

"Deon, wait! The baby's y—"

POP!

***

Canyon and Symba looked like a young Hollywood couple as they exited the Westin together hand in hand. They'd just had dinner and drinks at *Sundial* and were now on their way to the movies.

Although things were rocky in the beginning, they'd made a smooth transition as a unit. Symba couldn't have been any happier for finally taking a chance.

The valet had just pulled up with the custom Mercedes Benz Canyon brought for her when his cellphone suddenly rang. "Aye, what's up?" he answered, noticing Lamont had called the emergency business line.

Just then, several squad cars rushed onto the hotel's premises with their sirens blaring. Anxiously hopping out the car, one officer demanded for Canyon to drop his phone.

"Canyon, what's going on?" Symba asked in fear. She still had no clue what he did for a living.

She also didn't realize the Feds had been watching them for the last few weeks.

Before Canyon had a chance to respond, the cuffs were slapped on the both of them while their rights were read.

"Canyon?" Symba called out as she was led to a cruiser.

"Bay, don't say shit! I'ma call my lawyer and I'ma fix this shit. I promise!"

"Canyon, why is this happening?"

The door to the police car slammed in Symba's face after she was roughly shoved inside. She'd never been so afraid and confused in her life. *What have I gotten myself into*, she asked.

Suddenly, Symba didn't believe Canyon was a warehouse manager after all…

How foolish could I have been?

***

Raelyn tightened her cotton robe as she walked through the sliding glass doors back in her home. She could swim in the Olympic pool out back all day, but she knew that would be a stretch. Caesar's mini-mansion felt more like a retreat, and

Raelyn was privileged to call the place her new home. Drama and rent-free, she couldn't have been any happier with her new life and her new man.

"Did Maria stop over earlier?" Raelyn asked Caesar on the way to the kitchen. Maria was the Spanish Chef who prepared their meals daily.

"Yeah, she left somethin' in the fridge," Caesar told her, not looking up from his notebook. Sitting on an egg white sectional in the room beside the kitchen, he went over numbers. Though Caesar trusted his accountant, it never hurt to double check.

As soon as Raelyn walked into the kitchen, her jaw was met with the butt of a loaded Glock. After hearing her fall and hit the floor, Caesar tossed the notebook and rushed to the kitchen. Inside, he was met with the unexpected sight of three masked men carrying weapons.

Snatching his ski mask off, the apparent leader stepped forward. "First I'ma take everything you got in this mufucka," Jett said. "Then we gon' take a ride to yo' stash house, and I'ma cop everything in that bitch too."

Crying softly, Raelyn held her busted lip while cowering next to Caesar.

Jett laughed wickedly at how pathetic she looked next to the nigga. "Then I'ma take my bitch back and do what I should've done to yo' ass a long time ago."

TO BE CONTINUED…

ABOUT THE AUTHOR

Pebbles Starr discovered her passion for creative writing in elementary school. Born in 1989, she began writing poetry as an outlet. She then converted her poetry into short stories. Later on, as a teen, she led a troubled life which later resulted in her becoming a ward of the court.

Pebbles fell in love with the art and used storytelling as a means of venting during her tumultuous times. Aging out of the system two years later, she was thrust into the dismal world of homelessness. Desperate, and with limited income, Pebbles began dancing full time at the tender age of eighteen.

It wasn't until fall of 2008 when she finally caught her break after being accepted into Cleveland State University. There, she lived on campus and majored in Film and Television. Now, six years later, she flourishes from her childhood dream of becoming a bestselling author. To learn more, visit www.jadedpublications.com.

CPSIA information can be obtained
at www.ICGtesting.com
Printed in the USA
LVHW04s2003050718
582798LV00001B/184/P